THE ORGANIZATION

PREVIOUS BOOKS BY ALAN REFKIN

FICTION

Matt Moretti and Han Li Series

The Archivist
The Abductions
The Payback
The Forgotten

Mauro Bruno Detective Series

The Patriarch
The Scion
The Artifact
The Mistress

NONFICTION

The Wild Wild East: Lessons for Success in Business in Contemporary Capitalist China
By Alan Refkin and Daniel Borgia, PhD

Doing the China Tango: How to Dance around Common Pitfalls in Chinese Business Relationships
By Alan Refkin and Scott Cray

Conducting Business in the Land of the Dragon: What Every Businessperson Needs To Know About China
By Alan Refkin and Scott Cray

Piercing the Great Wall of Corporate China: How to Perform Forensic Due Diligence on Chinese Companies
By Alan Refkin and David Dodge

THE ORGANIZATION

BOOK ONE OF THE GUNTER WAYAN
PRIVATE INVESTIGATOR SERIES

ALAN REFKIN

THE ORGANIZATION
BOOK ONE OF THE GUNTER WAYAN
PRIVATE INVESTIGATOR SERIES

iUniverse books may be ordered through booksellers or by contacting:

iUniverse
1663 Liberty Drive
Bloomington, IN 47403
www.iuniverse.com
844-349-9409

ISBN: 978-1-6632-2315-9 (sc)
ISBN: 978-1-6632-2314-2 (e)

Library of Congress Control Number: 2021909985

Print information available on the last page.

iUniverse rev. date: 06/04/2021

To my wife, Kerry

To the aunts: Betty Fitch, Ann Schumacher,
Debby K. Jantz, in memory of Shari Orr,
in memory of Coleen Mammen,
in memory of Kaye Dorn

CHAPTER 1

T HE CHARRED AND broken piece of wreckage, no larger than the lid of a coffin, was gently undulating in the warm winter currents of the Indian Ocean. The semiconscious singed and bruised man atop the ragged piece of fiberglass was five feet, seven inches tall, had black hair, brown skin, and brown eyes that, under normal circumstances, were flat and expressionless. He wasn't athletic by any stretch of the imagination, shunning sports and exercise because his parents believed such pursuits were silly and wouldn't put money in his pocket. Whereas reading books and concentrating on schoolwork would get him a good job and a way to support a wife and family. As a result, he gained a small tire around his stomach at an early age that remained to this day.

The 33-year-old Balinese private investigator and former police detective had been afloat on the open sea without food or water for nearly three days. With the alternating heat of the day and the cold of night sucking the energy from his body, he had barely enough strength to grip the jagged piece of his boat that was preventing him from becoming part of the ocean's food chain. Casting a gaze at the sun slipping into the sea, which extinguished the last remnants of daylight, the man struggled to keep his eyes open. Eventually, the combination of dehydration, fatigue, and lack of food took its toll, and he closed his eyes and began the journey into an unconsciousness from which he would never recover. Seconds later, fate intervened.

The five feet, four inches tall nearly bald man was 75 years old. His skin was dark brown, wrinkled, and leathery - the result of both age and decades of exposure to the elements. His gnarly and callused hands, despite his age, had a grip that was not unlike a vice. A fourth-generation fisherman, he sat in the same ten-foot handmade wooden boat that his father and grandfather used. Casting his line into the water, he was pulling his favorite jig across the seagrass 12 feet below him, jerking the rod several times in quick succession, imitating the motion of a prawn before letting the jig come to rest. If a squid was near, they'd attack it. The old man had fished the waters off Uluwatu, Bali, since the age of 12, and he knew that the best time to catch the elusive cephalopods was a couple of hours before and after sunset. The six squids in his livewell were a testament to his knowledge and skill.

He was about to retrieve and recast his jig when something struck his craft with a dull thud. Believing it to be flotsam, which was common near shore, he put down his rod and took a flashlight from a plastic box, inspecting the side of his boat where he'd heard the impact. That's when he saw the unconscious man atop a jagged piece of fiberglass. Pulling him onto his boat, the old man slowly dripped water into his mouth until he saw his eyes open. Eventually, the rescued man became more alert and consumed the two bottles of water the old man had with him. The fisherman didn't have a phone. Therefore, after pulling in his line, he engaged his small outboard motor and steered his craft towards the nearest dock, which belonged to a hotel. He'd fished these waters all his life and, although the pier wasn't visible at night and he didn't own a navigational aid, one glance at the stars was all he needed to set his course. An hour later, the survivor was in a hospital.

As Gunter Wayan opened his eyes, the first thing he saw was a gorgeous brunette. Behind her was a circle of intensely bright light.

"Am I in heaven?" Wayan asked, his speech weak and slightly distorted. "You're so beautiful; you must be an angel."

The nurse smiled and stepped aside.

"Nothing wrong with his eyesight," the doctor standing behind the attractive woman quipped, pushing the examination light to the side as he and another person stepped forward.

"You had a close one," police captain Riko Dhani, who was standing to the right of the doctor, said. The officer was five feet, five inches tall, had green-grey eyes and salt and pepper hair cut so close to the scalp that it was stubble. He was husky but not muscular. Years of smoking yellowed his teeth, although he'd recently quit. As a habit, he never fastened his shirt's top button, even when wearing a tie because his neck was too large for the size shirt he purchased. He could buy a bigger shirt with a larger neck size. However, because of his tree-trunk neck and short stature, if he did it would look like he was wearing a kaftan and tucked it in.

"Where am I?" Wayan asked in a hoarse voice.

"In a hospital," Dhani answered.

"How did I get here?"

Dhani explained.

3

"Does Eka know?" referring to his assistant, Eka Endah.

"I called her. She's on her way," Dhani answered.

"Before you continue this conversation, I need to examine my patient and ensure he's up to it. Give us a few minutes," the doctor interjected, pulling the privacy drape around Wayan's bed to show there was no discussion on the matter.

Dhani went into the hall and sat in one of the green plastic chairs against the wall, waiting for the doctor to finish so that he could return and question Wayan. While he was waiting, Eka Endah arrived.

The five-foot, six-inch hazel-eyed statuesque woman had tawny brown skin, very shapely legs, ample breasts, and brunette hair cascading over her shoulders. She wore a short black dress and black high heels as she approached the police captain. Dhani did a doubletake. The woman in front of him was the butterfly who emerged from the cocoon. Prior to this, he'd only seen her in loose conservative clothing in Wayan's office.

"How is he?" Eka asked.

"Conscious. The doctor is examining him."

"I was at a girlfriend's party," she explained after seeing how Dhani looked at her.

"Wayan's my friend. But you know you could get a job in a heartbeat at a high-end resort. I'm guessing you'll make substantially more than what he's paying you. I could set the meetings."

"I like my job. Wayan's a good man who helps others who can't help themselves. Being a part of that gives me a great deal of satisfaction."

"Satisfaction, but not money. From what I hear, most of his clients don't have a pot to piss in."

"Wayan manages."

"He needs to join one of the Jakarta agencies which set up shop in Bali."

"He's a brilliant detective. He'll survive on his own."

"He is a brilliant detective. I should know; I was his partner. Today, people don't want a gumshoe like Wayan; they want a sophisticated approach to their investigative needs. I put in a word for him at several of these agencies. They told me they've called."

"He's turned down their job offers."

"Talk some sense into him, Eka. His woefully neglected vehicle requires major surgery if it's to survive, his credit is in the tank from the bills that have piled up, and his landlord, who's a friend of mine, is losing patience with his promises to pay the rent. However, I suspect an irregular paycheck doesn't bother you."

"I get by."

"Is there any truth to the rumor you were the sole beneficiary of your father's trust, which owned the land on which they built the airport? I heard the trust is sizeable."

"You seem unusually well informed regarding Wayan and me."

"I was a detective, even though I'm now the paper pusher overseeing detectives."

"Well, Captain Dhani, someone has solved Wayan's financial problems."

"You?"

"No. He won't accept my money. We have a new client who has a rather large pot to piss in."

Dhani frowned.

The doctor came out of the room and told the captain that he could return. Eka followed, startled when she saw her boss with bandages on his face and arms and sporting a black eye.

"You've got a visitor, Sam," Dhani said, using the nickname he'd given Wayan after discovering they both loved the movie Casablanca.

"How do you feel?" Eka asked.

"Well enough to go home."

"I expect you'll get pushback from the doctor, especially since you were unconscious and floating in the ocean less than eight hours ago," Eka said.

"What happened?" Dhani asked.

"Wrong place. Wrong time."

"Can you be more specific?" he asked, removing a notepad and pen from his jacket pocket.

"Someone hired me to rent a boat and rendezvous at a specific time with another craft 30 miles offshore. The other boat was to give me cardboard boxes to bring ashore."

"Drugs?"

"That's what I initially thought and why I at first turned down the job. However, in our next communication, my client explained the reason for the ocean rendezvous was that he was being watched. He wanted me to bring the boxes ashore and give them to someone. Addressing my concern about the contraband, he said that I could open any of the boxes and, if I found contraband, I could throw it into the ocean."

"If there's nothing illegal within the boxes, why doesn't the person you're meeting at sea pull into a marina and have them delivered to whomever?"

"I don't know."

"Your client doesn't trust FedEx or another reputable carrier? No offense, but they're reliable and much cheaper."

"I know."

"Did you look inside the boxes?"

"I never had the chance."

"Why?"

"Because all hell broke loose. The boat delivering them to me exploded 50 yards from my craft. In the light cast by the explosion, I saw a drone passing over it and coming towards me."

"A drone destroyed the other boat?"

"Yes. And it was large - one you'd expect the military to use."

"Were the boxes lost at sea?"

"If they were on the boat."

"Interesting. Keep going."

"I pushed the throttles on my boat to the stops, trying to get away from the burning debris and into the darkness ahead of me."

"You didn't make it."

"I couldn't outrun the drone. As it lined up behind me, I jumped into the ocean. A second later, a missile struck my boat. Flames from the explosion brushed over me, and I was hit in the eye by flying debris. Fortunately, a small piece of my craft was next to me, and I climbed onto it and floated for three days. You know the rest."

"Who's your client? I need to speak with them."

"I don't know who hired me. Even if I did, I couldn't tell you. It's privileged. You know that."

Dhani probed Wayan on what he believed was an inconsistency in what he told him. "You said that you spoke with your client and initially turned down the job because you believed you were transporting contraband. Therefore, you must know the identity of your client. Why are you saying you don't?"

"I never said I spoke with them. We have a procedure. I send my questions or whatever else I have to say to a post office box. They communicate with me by messenger. If they're this careful with me, I'm certain an intermediary goes to the post office box, and there's a separate procedure for them to communicate with my client - one that preserves their anonymity. That's the way I'd do it."

"Me too. Still, they hired you for a job that FedEx could perform. Something doesn't add up. Are you telling me everything?"

"Everything that's not privileged."

"Eka implied they paid you well."

"They did."

"Okay. Let's say there was no attack. You received the boxes, checked and verified no contraband was inside, and docked the boat. Was your client going to meet you at the dock?"

"I don't know if the client or someone else was going to meet me." Wayan lied, having rented a van and parked it at the dock. If the transfer at sea went as planned, he was to deliver the boxes to the person whose name and address his client sent him.

Dhani, frustrated with the answers that he received from his former partner, took a deep breath. "Why did he choose you?"

"I couldn't say. Obviously, a total lack of judgment."

"Forgive me for saying this, but you have reputational scars which are easily discovered. Yet, they chose you over the best investigative agencies in Indonesia, which have offices in Bali. Why?"

"Asked and answered," Wayan said, replying with a statement attorneys often use in depositions. "I don't know."

Is there anything else you want to tell me?"

"I'm going to find whoever tried to kill me, Riko. If I don't, the next time you and Eka see me, I'll be on a slab in the morgue."

CHAPTER 2

One day earlier

INDONESIA IS AN archipelago of over 13,400 islands between the Indian and the Pacific Oceans. With 268 million people, it's the fourth most populous country in the world. Many Indonesians believe that getting a legal degree is their ticket to respect and wealth. The road to attaining it is a three-step process. It first requires four to seven years of study after high school, successful completion of which confers a Bachelor of Law degree. The second step is an in-depth study of the country's laws. This gives the graduate the title of master in law. The third and final step continues the student's in-depth indoctrination into the law and addresses more complex legal issues and procedures. The time needed to complete the last two steps depends on how many courses someone elects to take per semester. In the end, no matter how long one takes, the goal of the three-step legal education system is to cram enough information into a student's head so they can pass the bar exam.

Rano Ishak was five feet, four inches tall. The chubby 27-year-old with unruly neck-length black hair knew he wasn't the sharpest pencil in the pack, nor an entire case of pencils. That was fine with him. He didn't attend law school with

11

altruistic or moralistic ideas. He regarded it as an investment that would lead to the wealth he'd always craved. Since his family could not pay for his legal education, he accumulated a great deal of debt getting to his career's starting line.

He was interested in corporate law, specifically setting up offshore corporations to hide wealthy clients' assets and understanding the intricacies of money laundering. He focused on these areas believing that the clientele who required these services would, by definition, be wealthy - and prosperous clients paid more legal fees than poor ones, especially for transactions that were on the shady side of legal.

In his last semester, law firms conducted on-campus interviews. They circulated lists, and students signed up to speak with the firms for which they wanted to work. The larger firms, which paid the most and offered the best benefits, had the entire graduating class to interview - except for one. Ishak eschewed them and placed his name on one interview sheet - a sole practitioner who had an unsavory reputation.

The rest of his class went to their interviews, looking like they belonged in GQ magazine. Ishak showed up wearing jeans and a black T-shirt - his everyday attire since he didn't own a suit or sports coat. During their two-hour conversation, the unsavory attorney's questions focused less on his legal acumen than his ethical propensities. Ishak was honest and shared his beliefs, which were on par with that of the unsavory attorney. His interviewer explained that his business had grown to where he needed to hire an attorney to supplement his two paralegals. Although he didn't offer Ishak a job, he did tell him to come to his office after graduation.

Upon receiving his diploma, Ishak went to the unsavory attorney's office and was offered a job on the spot, but at a nominal wage because he was there to learn the attorney's business practices while studying for the bar. It took four attempts to get his license to practice law, after which the unsavory attorney raised his salary, and he began meeting the firm's clients. Eight years later, his employer passed away from a heart attack. By that time, Ishak was as skillful as the unsavory attorney at setting up offshore corporations, cleaning and hiding money, and providing a vast array of illegal services for clients.

Inheriting the firm's business by default, Ishak contacted each client, most of whom already knew him. Ninety-five percent kept him as their attorney, and over the years, his reputation eclipsed that of his late employer, and his wealth increased exponentially.

Today, he received a text from one of his clients requesting three services. The first was to copy the 30 boxes of files that he stored at the law firm. Ishak billed a flat $10,000 per month storage fee and a $1,000 per hour service charge per paralegal to make copies of anything stored. His clients never argued about the cost. They kept sensitive information at the law firm because Ishak would invoke the attorney-client privilege if anyone wanted to inspect what they stored.

The second request was to rent a boat and place the copied files onboard. The client would send someone to captain the vessel, which they would return the following day. Ishak viewed these demands as part of the all-encompassing services he provided, for a fee, to a clientele who wanted their activities to be anonymous.

The third request directed him to sell his client's assets, at whatever the market would bear, and place the proceeds into an offshore entity that he created. Believing his client wanted to end his relationship with him, he sent a text, asking if this was his intent. The reply was terse: "I have terminal cancer.

Convert everything I own into cash and send the money to the designated offshore account. Subject closed."

Ishak rented a small cruiser and had the 30 boxes of copied papers loaded onboard. Phoning his client, he provided its location and slip number at a Jakarta marina.

Later that day, after contemplating how to make money from whomever his client worked for because he was greedy and losing business was something he didn't tolerate well, he went to the room where he stored client files. He removed a folder from a box that he selected at random, looked at the documents in it, and was satisfied they would suit his purpose. He next took the top folder from the box labeled *1-Administrative.* Opening it, he pulled the list within. He was familiar with the box, the folder, and the list because his client provided updates from time to time, requiring him to destroy the superseded list. The heading at the top of the first of the five pages was *The Organization.* Knowing that his client must be part of this entity because his name was on the list, and wanting an opportunity to establish a business relationship with them, he took a deep breath and phoned the person whose name appeared beside his client. He assumed she was his equal, associate, or replacement since his client was dying. She answered on the third ring.

"Who are you?" she asked without prelude since Ishak's phone did not provide his number.

He introduced himself.

"How did you get this number?"

Ishak told her it was in one of the boxes of files that he was storing for his client and was below her name on a list with the heading *The Organization.*

"Who's your client?" she asked in an authoritative voice.

"Amat Jalwandi."

"You've got my attention. You're calling me for a reason. What is it?"

Ishak was not a friendly person by nature, but the woman he spoke to made him look like Mr. Rogers by comparison.

Ishak responded that he copied the 30 boxes of documents he was storing for Jalwandi and delivered these to a boat for transport at his client's direction.

"What's in the boxes?"

Taking the folder that he'd removed from the random box, he read the first page to the woman. "Should I read another document?" he asked once he'd finished.

"That's unnecessary. Give me the name of the marina, boat, and slip number. I want those boxes and the originals."

"The boat may have already left, but I had a homing beacon installed so I could locate the cruiser if it ran into problems." He gave her the transmission frequency.

"Why are you doing this?"

"A good-faith gesture to establish my credibility with The Organization. In return, I wish to be your attorney and expect a finder's fee for the delivery of the original files."

"What's your idea of a finder's fee?"

"Twenty-million dollars wired to this account." Ishak provided the bank's name, account number, and routing information.

"Wait," she said, putting him on hold. Five minutes later, she returned and confirmed that she wired the money.

Ishak checked his offshore account, seeing he was $20 million richer.

"At nine tomorrow morning, a private aircraft will be at the Jakarta Soekarno-Hatta International Airport to transport you and the files you referenced to Bali. You'll receive a text providing the location and tail number of the aircraft. When we meet, we'll discuss your future services. In return for the money you received, every electronic device in your possession needs to be cleansed of Amat Jalwandi's name and any mention of the files you're transporting and that you copied. That includes computers, backups, phones, tablets, and so forth."

"Done. I should mention that I made a copy of the files I'm bringing to you and that it's in a secure location. Using a cliché, should anything happen to me, they'll be sent to the authorities."

"Understood," the woman responded in a monotonal voice before the line went dead.

Although there was no copy of the files other than what he'd made for his client, he felt his conversation with the woman gave the impression that mutually assured destruction would occur if any harm came to him. He viewed this threat as good business. Everyone just wanted to make money. Besides, he reasoned, no one wired $20 million to someone they intended to kill. He was wrong.

CHAPTER 3

Present day

G UNTER WAYAN'S RESIDENCE was a two-bedroom apartment in Pecatu, a region in Bali's southwestern peninsula known for its limestone cliffs and isolated small beaches that was popular with nudists. Besides voyeurists, Pecatu attracted surfers from all over the globe. Neither pursuit interested Wayan. He rented his apartment for sentimental reasons because he and his late wife lived there, and he refused to move. The clifftop apartment, which had a magnificent view of the Indian Ocean, was new when they moved in. Although two bedrooms was one too many for the couple, they someday planned to have children and turn the spare bedroom into a nursery.

Deciding to keep the apartment after losing his job as a police detective was a financial stretch, even though the newly self-employed investigator used it as both his residence and office. With a shortage of Bali apartments that overlooked the sea, the rent increased every year. However, emotion trumped reason, explaining to his assistant his fear that if he moved, the reminiscing memories of his wife that the apartment evoked would fade away.

Eka Endah parked her Range Rover Sport in front of the apartment building and accompanied Wayan into the elevator, pressing the button for the third floor. The apartment/office was to the left as they exited, and she unlocked the door.

"I'm fine," Wayan said. "Go home, and we'll catch up tomorrow." Opening the door, he saw an eight-by-ten-inch manila envelope on the floor - identical to the one he'd previously received from his unknown client. Eka bent down, picked it up, and handed it to him.

"You'd better come in," Wayan said as he went to the kitchen table and sat down. She closed the door and sat in the chair beside him. Tearing open the envelope, he found two $10,000 cashier's checks and a two-page note. He placed the pages of the note side by side between them.

I'm sorry for the mishap. Please accept $10,000 as my apology for your injuries. If you're willing, I would like you to take possession of a future shipment of boxes and deliver them - details to follow. I included a second check for that purpose. If you feel the risk is too significant, keep both checks as compensation for what occurred.

Please believe that I did everything to lessen the peril to you. Using hard copies of the information in the boxes you were to receive was a last resort. I explored getting the digital files, which could be arranged and categorized to make the data understandable. If I'd succeeded, you would have come to Jakarta and received a fob or hard drive. However, a trusted source told me that the computer system containing this information was inaccessible without a code from senior management.

I thought of having the person safeguarding my files photograph them. However, with 140,000 individual pages in 5,000 color-coded folders, it would not be easy to associate them with the proper folder to see the complex relationship between parties and the activities in which they are engaged. Therefore, copying was faster and made it easier to maintain the integrity of the data. I'm explaining this, so you know that I take your safety seriously. I will contact you when I receive confirmation that the next shipment of boxes is approaching the Bali shoreline. As always, discretion is paramount. Your life, my life, and everyone involved in this process is at risk.

The unsigned note was on copy paper, written with a bold hand in black ink. As with the first note, a messenger service, whose imprint was on the envelope, delivered it. Wayan previously went to their office and asked the dispatcher where they picked up the envelope. At first, the person refused to divulge anything but changed their mind when handed a wad of cash. With their now enhanced recall, they said the pickup was waiting for them on a park bench and, next to the envelope they were to deliver was one containing cash for the delivery, along with a generous tip.

"Sounds like our client wants to give it another try," Eka said. "How about you?"

"They should get something for their money. I need to rent a boat from another marina. I can't go back to the one whose vessel is charred debris floating on the Indian Ocean."

"Do you think?"

Wayan ignored the jab.

"The writing on this note is consistent with the first one. The bold heavy-handed style showing our client is confident, fearless, and a risk-taker," Eka added.

The first note Wayan received from the mystery client provided, besides the mechanics of delivering the boxes at sea, a post office box address for Wayan to communicate with him. It also gave the name, address, and phone number of the person he was to deliver the boxes - information he didn't disclose to Dhani because he didn't want the police involved until he sorted out what was happening.

"Can you deposit these?" Wayan asked, handing Eka the checks.

She said she would.

"I need to call the person to whom I was to deliver the boxes and tell them what happened. It's reasonable to assume that he and our client communicate, but I'll know for sure once I call."

Eka concurred it was a good idea.

He made the call. When the man answered, Wayan gave his name.

"Go ahead," the gravelly voice said.

"My boat, and the one delivering the boxes to me, were destroyed last night. The shipment is lost."

"I know. You'll have better luck next time. This is a burner phone. I'll send another contact number shortly. Anything else?"

When Wayan told him there wasn't, the call ended. "Not much of a conversationalist," Wayan said, putting his cell phone on the table.

"What did he say?"

"Do better next time."

"Since you almost died when he sent you to pick up the boxes, maybe it would be a good idea to take another stab at finding out the identity of our client before this next pickup to know what you're up against," Eka said.

"Good idea. Let's go over what we have. We know that an offshore corporation rented the post office box and paid for it a year in advance. That, if I didn't mention it before, was expensive to find out."

"This is the third time that you mentioned it. You also told me the address for this corporation was a bank in the Marshall Islands and that the contact information for the person renting the box was someone at that bank."

"We won't get their client's name from that person or the bank. The courier service which delivered the envelopes here said that they're paid to check the post office box daily and, if they find something inside, they call a number - almost certainly a burner phone."

"Let me guess. They deliver the contents of the PO box to a different location each time," Eka said.

"You got it. They leave whatever was in the box, pick up the envelope with the cash, and goodbye."

"Did they ever stick around to see who picked up what they left?" Eka asked.

"They said they didn't. I don't know if that's true. What I do know," Wayan said in a tired voice, "is that I need caffeine to keep it together. Do you want a coffee?"

Eka said she did.

Wayan got up and put a K-Cup of Lavazza Perfetto Espresso Roast Coffee in his Keurig and placed a black mug on the drip tray. He repeated the process with a second K-Cup, afterward handing a mug to Eka. Neither took anything in their coffee.

"What about Amat Jalwandi?" Eka asked. "You were to deliver the boxes to him. You have his address."

"I was thinking about that. As far as we know, besides you, me, and our client - he was the only one who knew where the boats would rendezvous. While you deposit the checks, I'll get changed and see what I can find on him. Give me the key to your car; I need to get the hospital bag with my clothes in them," Wayan said with a frown. He was still wearing his hospital gown and slippers.

"Do you mean the bag you grabbed after you disconnected your IV and walked out of the hospital with the angel, excuse me, nurse chasing you down the hall?"

"Dhani told you about the nurse?"

"He did."

"Yes, that bag."

"I tossed it in a trash receptacle in the parking garage after you handed it to me. Your clothes were singed, wet, and smelled. You weren't seriously going to wear them?"

"I was going to wash them first. It's my good luck outfit."

"All evidence to the contrary."

"I survived a drone attack."

"Barely. Take a shower, Wayan. Grab something else from your closet," Eka said as she picked up her car keys and the checks.

When Eka returned, she found Wayan dressed and sitting at his desk in the spare bedroom, which served as their office. Her desk was to the right of his.

"Anything on Amat Jalwandi?" she asked.

"Only background information - most of it coming from one article. If it weren't for that, he'd be a ghost. Why don't you look at what the government has," Wayan said, implying that she use the login and password given her by an admiring friend in the government, which permitted access to Indonesia's non-classified local and national government databases.

Eka agreed.

An hour later, they compared notes. Wayan started.

"Jalwandi is a 50-year-old former major general in the Indonesian army who retired six months ago. He has, as far as I can see, no social media accounts. After retirement, a newspaper article on him says he was born in Gianyar and spent four years at the Indonesian Military Academy, our equivalent of West Point, where he graduated as a second lieutenant. There's no evidence he's ever married or has children. That's all I have. What did you find?"

"His bank records show he has a modest sum of money in a savings account. The motor vehicle database indicates that he owns a black Nissan Terra, which is a four-door SUV. I have its license plate number. His house corresponds with the address where you were to deliver the boxes. Real estate records show a 4,300 square foot structure with three bedrooms, three bathrooms, and two swimming pools. One side of the house has an ocean view through floor-to-ceiling windows. He bought it with cash six months ago for $842,000."

"Just after he retired?" Wayan stated. "Not bad for someone who was on military pay."

"Let's speak with him. Our client hasn't given you the time or place to pick up the boxes. I could be a while."

"Good point. You drive. My Mahindra is a little iffy."

"I've heard."

It was 31 miles from Pecatu to Gianyar. Driving anywhere in Bali was a test of patience. Most roads were two lanes, packed, and weaved through the island's small towns and villages, making the going slow. Motorcycles, mopeds, and bicycles intertwined with this anemic procession. The result was that it took one and a half hours to get to Jalwandi's residence.

"Nice house," Eka said, parking the Range Rover 100 yards away and beside the two-lane road that ran by the residence and paralleled the ocean.

"It looks like they cleared the jungle to build this place but kept a dense untamed piece of it on either side."

"The general doesn't have to worry about being on top of his neighbors."

"I don't know what a major general's retirement pay is, but the upkeep and taxes alone might stretch the rubber band for a retired military officer."

Eka didn't reply. She reclined her seat slightly, activated the back massage, and turned the seat heater to its lowest setting.

Wayan, who was still hurting from the explosion, had an admiring look on his face as he saw what she did. "I don't suppose the passenger side has the same creature comforts?"

"Sit back," she said, adjusting his seat settings to duplicate hers.

Their massage continued for two hours until the main gate to Jalwandi's residence opened, and his black Nissan darted into the street. Eka fired up the Rover and followed.

Jalwandi drove to an outdoor farmers market approximately three miles from the residence and parked. Seconds later, Eka pulled into a parking space 50 yards away, and Wayan got out of the vehicle and followed the retired general.

"That was a bust," Wayan said 20 minutes later as he climbed back into the Rover and closed the door.

"Did he speak with anyone?" Eka asked, watching Jalwandi getting into his vehicle.

"He spoke with several merchants, but only long enough to pay for what he bought."

"What did he buy?" Eka asked as she pulled out of the parking lot and followed the Nissan. They were headed back towards the residence.

Wayan removed a notepad from his pocket and began reading. "A bag of rice, a half carton of eggs, several cloves of garlic, fresh chicken, an onion, fresh chili, and kecap manis, or sweet soy, depending on what you want to call it."

"He's making nasi goreng."

"He was shopping for dinner. I hope he brings a hot plate of it to us. I'm starving," Wayan said as Eka returned to the same surveillance spot they previously occupied and turned off the engine. She reinstituted their massages.

Forty-five minutes later, they heard a sharp tap on the driver's side window. Turning to their left, they saw the unsmiling face of a five-foot, ten-inch-tall man who was approximately 50 years old. He had salt and pepper hair cut close to the scalp, black opal eyes, and light brown skin. He was pointing a handgun at them.

"Both of you - get out of the car," he ordered.

After they complied, he directed them to an open dark green gate that, when closed, visually blended into the heavy foliage on the residence side of the road. Passing through the gate, the man pointed to the side door of the house, which led to the kitchen.

"Into the other room," he ordered.

Following his directions, they entered the view room, whose floor-to-ceiling windows looked out to the ocean.

"Why are you two following me?" Amat Jalwandi asked, keeping his gun trained on them.

"We're looking for answers."

"To what?"

"Who tried to kill me, and how were they able to get a missile-carrying drone to carry out the attack? Why did they want to destroy the boxes I was to deliver to you? Those are just for starters," Wayan said, not fazed by the weapon aimed at them. "Only four people knew about the delivery at sea. Two are on this side of the gun, the other is my client, and you're the fourth - the person to whom we were to make the delivery. That makes you the likely source of the leak."

"I'm not the leak; I'm your client," Jalwandi said as he laid his gun down on a side table. "I didn't have a photograph of either of you, or I would have invited you inside earlier - although not at gunpoint."

"You saw us?" Wayan asked.

"Through those binoculars," he said, pointing to a pair on the side table.

"You hired us to deliver your boxes to you?" Wayan asked in disbelief.

"From my attorney to me."

"Please fill in the blanks," Eka said, "because your attorney or a messenger service could have sent them to you directly. This makes no sense."

"It will once I explain. Are you hungry?"

"Famished," Wayan replied.

"I made nasi goreng. I always cook enough so I can have leftovers. Let's go into the kitchen and talk." Without waiting for a response, he led the way.

They followed him to a round table where he set two more places before breaking three eggs onto a large skillet. As they were cooking, he scooped the nasi goreng from a large pot on the stove onto three plates. Once the eggs were over easy, he put one atop each helping of nasi goreng and brought the food to the table.

"Start eating while I get us something to drink," Jalwandi said. He went to the refrigerator, took out three bottles of Bintang, Indonesia's most popular beer, removed the caps, and placed a bottle beside each plate. "You've probably done your research on me before you came."

Eka said they did.

Jalwandi sat down and took a sip of the pale lager. "Let me tell you a little about me, some of which you may already know. I recently retired after a 30-year career in the army, having never married or had children. I love this area of Bali because I grew up in a house several miles away," he said, pointing to his left. "You're probably wondering how it's possible to buy such an expensive residence on a military salary. It isn't. The money to purchase it came from the inheritance my parents left me as their only child. Since I know little about finance, I asked the Jakarta firm which managed their money to manage mine. They did very well."

"That checks a couple of boxes," Wayan said. "Why did you pick me for this job? You didn't even know what I looked like."

"Do you remember Major Langit Tamala?"

"A military officer accused of murder two years ago, when I was a police detective."

"You have an excellent memory. What else do you recall?"

"He became a suspect because of an anonymous tip from a purported witness. The caller said he saw the major argue with someone in a bar and that he followed them when they left and continued their dispute on the beach. This supposed witness also said he saw Major Tamala kill that person and rifle through the man's pockets and steal his money clip and the cash it held before running off."

"This caller must have known Major Tamala if they gave his name," Eka added.

"That was my assumption," Wayan answered.

"And you arrested the major?" Eka asked.

"It wasn't my case. The two detectives assigned to it went to the army base and searched his room. They arrested him after they found the victim's money clip on his desk."

Wayan took a sip of beer and attacked his nasi goreng.

"How were you involved?" Eka asked.

Wayan answered as he chewed his meal. "Detectives are overworked and try to resolve a case as quickly as possible, stopping when they believe they have enough evidence to give to the prosecutor so they can get a conviction. They then pick up the next folder from the stack on their desk and begin or continue that investigation. I got involved because one of the detectives on this case wanted me to look at their package before they submitted it to see if they'd missed anything. This was a common practice among detectives as a fresh set of eyes might pick up on something that was overlooked. No one wants to be embarrassed by having the prosecutor bounce a case back to the department."

"What did you find?" Eka continued.

"Several things didn't add up. The entire case revolved around the money clip and a tipster who never identified themself or came forward. This supposed witness said that the victim had a sizeable amount of cash in this money clip, which the bartender confirmed because they saw the victim peel off several bills from it. Major Tamala had $20 in his pocket when they arrested him, and they found no other money in his room."

THE ORGANIZATION

Eka, who'd never heard this story, pushed her bowl to the side and stared intently at Wayan.

"Another inconsistency involved the crime scene, which was the beach behind the bar. The medical examiner gave the time of death as an hour after sunset. This raised two questions, the most obvious of which was how the witness saw the murder and the money clip because the area, which was devoid of lighting, was dark. Also, what was the victim doing on the beach?"

"Did you find the answers?" Eka asked.

"More a theory than answers. I believe the victim wanted to speak to someone where nobody could hear their conversation. Otherwise, why leave the bar and stay in the area? The investigating detectives discovered the local beach authority raked the area just before sunset to prepare for the following day. The crime scene photos showed the only footprints besides those of the deceased were from someone wearing New Balance athletic shoes who walked parallel to the victim. Because of the even spacing of their pace, I believe that the victim and the individual next to him were having a nonviolent conversation."

Wayan explained that when they arrested Tamala, he was wearing boots. They found a pair of Nike shoes in his barracks locker, which didn't have a single grain of sand embedded in the soles. Instead, they had compressed dirt and small grass clippings wedged in them.

"But that wasn't what freed Tamala, was it?" Jalwandi said, leading Wayan to the finish line.

"No. It was the autopsy report the coroner issued two days after the murder. It concluded the victim died from a knife wound to the heart. That wasn't a hard conclusion to reach since the killer left the knife, devoid of fingerprints, embedded in the victim. The coroner also concluded that the assailant was right-handed and approximately five feet, five inches tall, one inch shorter than the victim. He came to that decision because the knife entered the body at a slight upward angle. Tamala was six feet, five inches tall, and left-handed. If he were the killer, the knife would have impacted the victim with a downward thrust."

"The money clip was a setup," Eka said.

"The murderer or one of his accomplices slipped it into Tamala's pocket at the bar after lifting it off the victim. Tamala, wondering how the clip got in his pocket, said he put it on his desk when he emptied his pockets that night."

"Who was the victim?" Eka asked.

"Someone who had a gambling habit. Remember when I said that, as soon as a detective has enough for the prosecutor to get a conviction, they'll stop investigating?"

Eka said she did.

"In reviewing the package that the case detectives gave me, the information on the victim was thin. They never looked into his background because they felt they had an airtight case against Major Tamala. I asked one of my snitches what the street knew about the victim. He said he owed a lot of money to the wrong people. Moreover, he'd told just about everyone that he was leaving Indonesia for a friendlier country - not the brightest thing to do. Add everything up, and even a rookie defense attorney would shred the prosecution's case. After I gave my findings to the lead detective, the department dropped the investigation."

Langit Tamala was one of my commanders in the Kopassus, the army's special forces group. He was a good soldier. At times, he drank a little too much, but so do we all," Jalwandi said.

"Was?" Wayan asked, picking up on the past tense.

"He was on the boat carrying the boxes. He would always do a favor for a friend - no questions asked."

"I could have delivered the boxes directly to you from wherever they originated. Why the intrigue? Why use Major Tamala?" Wayan asked, the irritation evident in his voice.

"I didn't want you to open up boxes looking for contraband and read what was in my files. Since they divulge a host of illegal activities, you might have turned them over to the authorities instead of delivering them to me. That would have severely impacted my plans."

"That's why you asked Major Tamala to take the boxes from Jakarta to a point off the coast?"

"Yes. You know Major Tamala, and there's trust between the two of you. I would expect you to open several of the boxes during the transfer to verify that no contraband was inside, but at sea and in the darkness of night, you wouldn't have time to peruse many of the files, if any. You would have had an abundance of time in Jakarta."

"That doesn't explain why Major Tamala couldn't go another 30 miles to shore and deliver the boxes to you."

"I believe my former associates are watching my residence. Yesterday, I saw with my binoculars that someone was in the dense vegetation some distance from the house. They weren't visible for long and were far better at concealment than the both of you."

Wayan frowned at Jalwandi, showing he didn't appreciate that statement, however accurate it might be.

"If I was being watched," Jalwandi continued without pause, "and he delivered the files here, they would believe we're working together and that what was in the boxes related to them - which it did. Given the attack on the boats, someone in The Organization found out about the transport of the files, saw the major picking up the boxes in Jakarta, followed his boat, saw yours, and preemptively eliminated the uncertainties by destroying the boxes and killing everyone. Almost everyone, Jalwandi corrected."

"Explain what you meant by The Organization?" Eka asked.

"Later."

"But, unlike the major, I was expendable," Wayan stated in a voice that showed he was pissed.

"You have a keen sense of survival, which is undeniable because you're here and not floating on the Indian Ocean. Also, your police training taught you how to deal with the dark side of life better than a combat soldier who knows only military tactics and the battlefield. Wayan, you're difficult to kill and are a formidable adversary for any opponent. To answer your earlier statement - you're only expendable if someone can kill you. I believed you would survive, and Tamala wouldn't."

"I assume the note you sent, saying that you cared for my safety, was bullshit to draw me into accepting a second rendezvous at sea."

"I don't know how the leak occurred or who it might be. Therefore, there's no way to tell if they've learned about this second shipment. I desperately need the contents of those boxes for my plan to succeed. I had a feeling you wouldn't turn down my offer because, from what I understand of your personality after looking into your background and speaking with others, taking something for nothing goes against your ethics. Offering to let you keep the money for doing nothing was my way of having you stay in the game and help me."

"Your psychobabble is giving me a headache. The bottom line is that you're right. I won't take money for services I haven't performed, and I don't like to lose. Did you realize when you hired me that my departure from the force wasn't voluntary? They fired me for stealing a great deal of money."

"For taking $5,000 from a stack of $2 million in a raid at a drug dealer's home. You used it to pay for an experimental cancer treatment for your late wife that the insurance company wouldn't cover. If the person who turned you in had been under my command, he'd be shoveling shit out of latrines until retirement."

"What was worth Major Tamala's life and almost getting me killed?" Wayan asked after draining the last of his beer. "What are you planning to do with the files?"

"Use them for extortion."

CHAPTER 4

"**W**HAT IS THE Organization?" Eka asked for the second time.

"It's a multi-billion-dollar secret enterprise established by three individuals. It acts as an intermediary in laundering cash for North Korea, and owns multiple businesses throughout Asia, legitimate and not, which are too numerous to name."

"Who are the three founders?"

"Kulon Sanadi, Hulin Chao, and Min Kang."

Wayan and Eka said they were unfamiliar with the names.

"The Organization and its founders take great pains to remain anonymous. Sanadi is a retired Indonesian army general who was a paper pusher rather than someone who would lead a charge against a fortified position. He's a genius at logistics, administration, and finance. By finance, I mean money laundering and hiding assets. He retired from the military six years ago and lives in Hong Kong."

"Is he the person who got you involved with this illicit enterprise?" Wayan asked.

"He did. We've known each other for over 20 years."

"Chao sounds like a Chinese name," Eka said.

"Hulin Chao is a general in China's People's Liberation Army. Although he lives in Beijing, the Chinese government gave him the responsibility and resources to assist North Korea in laundering money by funneling their hidden revenue through Chinese and Hong Kongese companies and financial institutions. From there, it went to The Organization to be laundered."

"Chao must work closely with Sanadi," Wayan added. "That explains why Kulon Sanadi lives in Hong Kong. It's the perfect venue for The Organization's sleight of hand with China."

"You're connecting the dots. They also gave Chao a second responsibility. He's the military division commander that protects northwest China - their border with Pakistan, India, Nepal, the various stans, and so forth. This region includes Xinjiang, which has a population of 22 million - half of which are Muslim. His deputy runs the day-to-day operations, but he has the title of commander."

"You would think that his money laundering responsibilities would take all of his time," Eka said. "He lives in Beijing. Why a division commander in northwest China?"

"He's Beijing's problem solver. They assigned him this command after the Uyghur attacks in Tiananmen Square. Following his establishment of reeducation camps for Uyghurs, which are essentially prisons, everyone in the region became terrified of him."

"He sounds like someone you don't want to screw with," Wayan said.

"Stay as far away from him as possible."

"And Min Kang?" Eka asked. "Korean?"

"He's a four-star general in the North Korean army and Kim Jong-un's point person for money laundering."

Jalwandi explained Kang was aggressive, impulsive, narcissistic, devoid of compassion, and had no respect for human life. "Put him ahead of Chao as someone you don't want to screw with."

"Did The Organization order the drone attack that killed Major Tamala?" Wayan asked.

"I don't doubt they did. General Chao has access to the PLA's Soaring Dragon drone and has used it in the past against adversaries. When he takes a drone off the reservation, borrowing a line from the Americans, Chao alters its flight and weapons expenditure logs to show he used it in the northeast region to deal with civil disobedience, smuggling, or whatever story he concocts."

"Here's what I don't understand," Wayan said. "Chao and Kang are active general officers in the military. How do they have the time to manage The Organization? Second question: how can they take, what must be a great deal of money, and funnel it to an entity they own without North Korea or China finding out?"

"First, at the general officer level, almost everything is delegated. Therefore, finding time to manage their functions within The Organization wasn't difficult. Second, China and North Korea expect to pay a fee for money laundering and running their illegal activities. The ten percent that The Organization charges is the industry standard and what both countries paid before they came along. What neither country knows is that those running their laundering operations also wash the cash and keep the fees."

"If China and North Korea found out, they would want that money back," Eka added.

"Exactly. Neither country believed it possible to establish and maintain a cleaning operation of this magnitude without the United States finding out. Chao and Kang maintain this illusion."

"And if either country discovered that Chao and Kang lied?" Eka continued.

"They'd be killed, along with anyone who took part in this scheme."

"And you're extorting money from The Organization to keep that secret?" Wayan asked.

"Not only keeping it secret from China and North Korea, but also the United States, United Nations, and the governments of countries where they operate."

"You said Kulon Sanadi got you into The Organization. What was your position?" Wayan asked.

"I oversaw their Indonesian operations."

"Why do they focus on recruiting military officers?"

"They don't. Only the upper echelons have a concentration of current and former military. The founders believe that not only can military officers keep a secret, but their access to military, government, and police databases is invaluable."

"I'm curious. What did you do for them in Indonesia?" Wayan asked.

"I significantly expanded organ harvesting - legal and illegal. With Indonesia being the fourth most populous country in the world, we provide more organs for transplants than any Asian nation except China. Domestically, these are implanted in wealthy Indonesians or organ-recipient tourists. If neither of these groups can use a harvested organ, we go to the transplant database for Asia and contact the medical or private facility with an outstanding request. Organ harvesting money is laundered and funneled to North Korea. The Organization, as I said, gets a ten percent fee."

"If I understand this correctly, The Organization doesn't own these facilities; they manage them."

"That's correct."

"Why?"

"The Organization set up these operations for North Korea. In return, we receive two fees - one for management and the other to wash the cash."

"Why not get 100 percent?" Eka asked.

"We're large and formidable, but we wouldn't last long against the resources that North Korea or China could employ against us. If these two countries want to be in this business, they're going to be. It's better to have them as allies and make $275 million per month than engage in a clandestine war against them that is, in the end, unwinnable."

"Say that number again," Eka asked in a disbelieving tone."

"The Organization nets $275 million per month, $170 million of which is their fee for laundering the approximately $1.7 billion per month of the annual $20 billion in illicit revenue North Korea receives from organ harvesting, arms sales, and other activities not in compliance with various embargos. The remaining $100 million-plus is from their investments in legal and illegal enterprises that don't conflict with businesses they manage for the North Korean or Chinese governments."

"The Organization may be as big as PT Freeport," Eka added, referring to the copper and gold miner that was Indonesia's largest company.

"They're bigger. PT Freeport has net profits of around $870 million per year. I have stock in the company and see their annual reports. The Organization has an annual cash flow of $3.3 billion."

"How much of that money comes from organ harvesting?"

"Approximately $1.2 billion."

"You're a scumbag," Eka said with a look of disgust.

"I'm a dying scumbag who has between one and two months of life remaining before the pancreatic cancer that permeates my body puts me in the ground. However, for the record, I want you to know that the story about receiving my parent's inheritance and buying this house is true."

"You could have bought a much larger property," Wayan said.

"That would raise too many eyebrows. However, the vacations I've taken would make a Russian oligarch envious."

"Explain why you want to extort money from The Organization if it enabled you to live so well and you're dying," Wayan said. "Were the boxes Major Tamala was transporting the documented proof you mentioned earlier? Was it evidence that could bring down The Organization?"

"Yes to both questions. The boxes contained copies of tens of thousands of documents that I accumulated on their activities, along with a chart showing its operational structure by nation and the contact information for those involved."

"How much were you looking to extort?"

"I offered to give them the contents of the boxes for $100 million. As proof, I sent them a sampling of what I had."

"I'm sure that set them off," Wayan said.

"They were cathartic with anger and made a concerted effort to find and destroy the originals and any copies I may have made. One day, I came home and found my house ransacked and my computer was gone. The same thing happened to my friends and acquaintances. They somehow found out about the boxes that Major Tamala was bringing to you. When I heard you were in the hospital, I informed Sanadi that he only destroyed copies of what I had and doubled my demand to $200 million."

"If they knew about the shipment, they might know where you keep the originals," Wayan continued.

"I don't think so."

"How do you know?" Wayan asked.

"Because I'm still alive."

"Why are they going to all this trouble? If they're as ruthless as you imply, why don't they torture you to get the location of the originals and other copies you may have? That handgun will not deter a professional," Wayan said, looking at the weapon that Jalwandi previously pointed at them.

"I'm too sick to torture. My body will shut down 15 minutes into whatever they try. Plus, they know I'm a vindictive sonofabitch and, since I'm dying anyway, will lie and deceive them until my last breath. They'll get exactly zero from interrogating me. They'll pay me the money."

"Why would they waste $200 million?" Eka asked.

"It's a pittance compared to $3.3 billion and keeping China and North Korea from finding out their secret."

"Let's take a step back," Wayan said. "You're dying. You're rich. In the time you have left, why go to all this trouble to extort money? What can you do with $200 million in the time you have left?"

"Give it and the boxes to various governments."

Wayan and Eka gave Jalwandi an uncomprehending stare.

"I'm a criminal and, as this lovely lady accurately pointed out, a scumbag. I was morally weak. The money they offered for the first year of helping them was more than I made in my entire military career. I went off the rails, got ensnared by my greed, and became a different person. I didn't like that person. Finding out you're going to die redefines one's goals and forced me to answer two questions."

"And what would those be?" Eka asked.

"How to protect my country. North Korea's game plan is to surreptitiously buy large businesses, such as mining and aerospace, through legitimate enterprises they control. This allows them to have significant political influence because of the jobs and tax revenue. They'll also continue to expand their illegitimate endeavors, such as human trafficking and drugs, to name two. If Asian governments don't wake soon and see what's happening, the money generated from these endeavors will facilitate the expansion of North Korea's nuclear arsenal, fleet, and air force. Asia will be a powder keg, and North Korea will be the bully on the street. This will harm my country."

"Something you knew or should have known."

"As I said, I was greedy and became a different person. I can't unring that bell."

"And the second question you forced yourself to answer?" Wayan asked.

"The legacy I want to leave in this life. I want to be remembered for my military service and what I'm about to do. Hopefully, that will override the sins of the past."

"You want to regain your respect," Eka said.

"I want to regain my honor - the invisible badge I had for decades in the army."

"You said that you wanted to give the information you collected on The Organization, along with what's in the boxes, to various governments. Give me the mechanics of that," Wayan asked.

"The $200 million will go into a trust that I set up with a legitimate attorney. He'll also receive the boxes of information that I've collected. The files will be distributed to Asian countries where The Organization operates, giving proof of the illegalities they perpetrated. The money will pay the legal fees necessary to investigate and prosecute them. Without these, it's doubtful any Asian nation would have the proof or monetary resources to defeat The Organization in their country."

"And if you gave the cash to the various governments directly, they'd fritter it away because, if there's one thing that a government does well, it's waste money," Eka added.

"Well said."

"Have you ever thought that nothing would change because North Korea and China will replace The Organization and that the illegal enterprises and money laundering will continue unabated?" Wayan asked.

"I've considered that, and changes will occur. The information within those boxes will expose every legitimate and illegitimate investment North Korea has. It will indicate how they avoid sanctions, with General Chao's help, and the shell companies and financial institutions he uses to receive and launder their money."

"Did it ever occur to you that your attorney might have been the one to inform The Organization?" Eka asked. "I know you said that, because you're still alive, they didn't have the originals. But are you certain he didn't turn you in?"

"It's possible but unlikely. Again, because we're both alive. If he turned over the originals to The Organization, they'd kill both of us to make certain that whatever we knew went to the grave with us. Let's go into the other room; it's more comfortable. I have a bottle of 50-year-old Macallan scotch that I'm eager to consume before my death. You both can help. Leave the dishes."

Pinpointing the impact point on a target standing ten feet behind slanted sheets of glass requires a skilled shooter who must compensate for many variables that affect the track of their shot. This includes the type and thickness of the glass, its slant, the angle at which the bullet impacts it, the shooter's distance from the glass, how far the target is behind it, and the type of bullet used. Here, the floor-to-ceiling windows that looked out to the ocean slanted inward to give an architectural flare.

To the sniper, who looked closely at the windows when the owner briefly left home to get dinner, the slant meant that the bottom of the bullet would impact slightly before the top. Therefore, to hit his target, he would need to aim high. The shot was even more difficult with the intended victim ten feet behind the windows as the difference between hitting or missing the target was determined by micro-adjustments to his aim. Most snipers didn't have the skill to make this type of kill. Instead, they would put a round through the glass to break it and then follow with the money shot. However, the problem with this approach was that, depending on the time between shots, the target could involuntarily move upon hearing the glass break or dive to the ground.

The shooter on the dark beach, who stood 100 yards from the residence and looked at Jalwandi standing behind his ocean-view windows, was an ex-military sniper and expert marksman. Extending the tripod on his rifle, he assumed a prone position behind his weapon and opened his legs as wide as he could to help absorb his gun's recoil. After pressing the butt of his rifle to his shoulder and using the chicken-wing method, which was flapping his arm like a chicken to secure it in place, he adjusted the turrets, or knobs, on his scope.

The first adjustments were to the ocular and the magnification - to get his target in focus. He followed by aligning the parallax to bring his mark into the same focal plane as the reticle or crosshairs. Therefore, if his eye moved in relation to the scope, the reticle wouldn't move on the target. Although this adjustment wasn't needed for targets less than 250 yards away, the sniper nevertheless went down every item on a checklist that he'd committed to memory while in the military.

He next adjusted the elevation, ensuring that his point of aim would be the same as the point of impact. Since bullets fall as soon as they leave the rifle's barrel, he turned the scope's elevation turret counterclockwise to compensate for this drop. His hand then automatically went to the windage turret. Because the ocean breeze was from left to right, he turned the turret forward - away from him. This adjusted his aim to the left.

With the target in the center of the reticle, and standing still, he pressed the buttstock of the rifle firm against his face and applied four pounds of pressure to the trigger.

As Jalwandi was starting a toast, he was thrown backward, slamming into the cabinet behind him. Instinctively, Wayan lunged at Eka and pulled her to the floor. As he did, two rounds passed close enough for them to hear a whizzing noise as the bullets flew past.

"Crawl into the kitchen," Wayan shouted.

Eka, who saw Jalwandi's lifeless body several feet from her, didn't ask questions.

Once in the kitchen, they stood and ran out the side door and down the stairs. At the bottom, Eka started to go left, towards the gate and their vehicle. Wayan grabbed her arm and pulled her in the opposite direction - towards the dense jungle-like area beside the residence. Entering the ten-foot wall of tangled vegetation - they went far enough back to remain hidden but close enough to see anyone approaching. They waited in silence. It wasn't long before they saw a man, in the dim light cast off by the kitchen, running down the stairs. In his hands, he was holding a rifle.

The sniper was rail-thin, six feet, two inches tall, and had a skull-like face that seemed hollowed and wasted. As the man stepped in front of the wall of tangled vegetation, Wayan and Eka watched him raise his weapon and look through the scope of his rifle, moving the gun from their right to left, examining the vegetation. Wayan and Eka slowly crept backward until they could no longer see the man, Wayan figuring that if they couldn't see him, then he couldn't see them. He was right. After holding perfectly still for almost 30 seconds, they heard the sniper walk away. They continued to remain motionless. Less than a minute later, there was a screech of tires as a car sped away.

Leaving the jungle, Wayan and Eka went back inside. There was no need to check if Jalwandi was alive, the hole in the middle of his forehead put that issue to rest. Looking to their right, they saw that one of the window panels was shattered, letting in the ocean breeze.

"Whoever killed him was trained by the military," Wayan said. "That shot required a level of skill far beyond what you'd see from someone in the police department or a homegrown assassin."

"We were lucky."

"Absolutely. From what Jalwandi told us, The Organization either got the original files from the attorney's office or believed that he was a loose cannon and too big of a risk to let live until the pancreatic cancer killed him."

"Where does that leave us?" Eka asked.

"In the crosshairs of The Organization which, because they don't know what Jalwandi told us, wants us dead," Wayan said, removing the phone from his pocket.

"Who are you calling?"

"Dhani. The police need to be notified."

"And then what?"

"We try to stay alive long enough to figure out how to get the targets off our backs."

"Any idea how we do that?"

"None."

CHAPTER 5

K IM JONG-UN'S PRESIDENTIAL compound at Ryongsong
was one of eight residences the dictator maintained in
and around Pyongyang. An extensive tunnel system
connected each, with entry restricted to all but a few of
the dictator's closest advisors. Constructed in 1983 by the
country's first leader, Kim Il-sung, the Ryongsong palace
contained an underground wartime headquarters replete with
conference rooms, offices, and sophisticated communications
systems - compliments of the Chinese government. Covering
the thick concrete walls, which were embedded with layers
of rebar, was a sheathing of lead to protect those within from
radiation in the event of a nuclear attack.

The Ryongsong compound didn't suffer from a lack
of luxuries. Within the ten-foot-high electrified fence
surrounding it was a series of manufactured lakes, recreational
facilities, a shooting range, horse stables, a riding area, a
horse racing track, a running track, and an athletic field.
Directly behind the palace was a 160-foot-long, 49-foot-wide
swimming pool with a waterslide.

Security was tight. The area surrounding Ryongsong
was ringed by a ten-foot-high electrified fence. Between it
and the interior perimeter road that paralleled the fence was

an extensive minefield. Paranoid about his security, Kim Jong-un supplemented the vast number of military personnel already guarding the palace with two strategically positioned military encampments. Vehicles entering the compound went through a series of three checkpoints. A quarter-mile beyond the last was the presidential palace.

At six feet, one inch tall, General Min Kang was eight inches taller than the average North Korean, sometimes appearing to be even taller because of his ramrod-straight posture. The 54-year-old four-star was thin, had close-cropped salt and pepper hair, and dark brown eyes. His uniform was always crisp, and his shoes mirror-polished thanks to a corporal in the KPA, or Korean People's Army, who served as his valet.

Kang's government title was Director of Strategic Monetary Planning - which obfuscated the actual function of his office, which was to funnel foreign money into the cash-starved nation, bypassing the sanctions and embargoes placed on it. Given the acute demand for funds required to purchase the parts and equipment necessary to expand its missile and nuclear development programs, buy weaponry to protect the homeland, and purchase the luxury goods demanded by the Supreme Leader, Kang was always scrounging for cash and could not afford even the slightest hiccup in his existing cashflow streams. Working with General Chao and Kulon Sanadi, he was so far able to satisfy these monetary demands.

He was seated at the conference room table in Kim Jong-un's subterranean office for the weekly meeting of the country's governmental hierarchy and others whose input the supreme leader valued. The discussion followed an established protocol. After saying a few words to begin the session, Kim

Jong-un asked those seated around him, starting with the person to his left and continuing in a clockwise direction, to provide an update on the projects and assignments they'd been given. Kang went last, giving him a chance to hear the cash needs of those at the table, because that was the continuing challenge that confronted everyone in attendance.

There were five ways Kang got hard currency for the Hermit Kingdom - all of which needed to be washed by The Organization. The first came from legal and illegal organ harvesting. Although this network focused on Asia, Kang earlier told Kim Jong-un that they were quickly reaching a plateau where growth would be minimal because the number of legal and illegal donors had leveled off. Therefore, he asked and received permission to enter the Baltic states, where his research showed donors would be plentiful.

The second way Kang generated revenue was through human trafficking - exporting slave laborers to Russia and China. However, he could only sell around 100,000 people annually because the supreme leader needed 2,600,000 slaves to work in the nation's labor camps. Given the high mortality rates within the camps, he believed it doubtful that he could increase the export of laborers without expanding beyond Asia. Again, he had asked and received permission to enter the Baltic states, where his research showed an abundance of laborers.

The third method involved using front companies in Africa to manufacture arms and ammunition. Chao found this an efficient way to bypass United Nations sanctions since these products weren't for export but sold in the country of manufacture.

The fourth cash-generating activity was the manufacture and sale of drugs. These ranged from the non-addictive, such as Viagra, which replicated what Pfizer produced and sold globally, to methamphetamine and Captagon - the brand name for the synthetic stimulant fenethylline.

The last cash generator was cybercrime, where hackers penetrated financial institutions and cryptocurrency exchanges.

When it came time for Min Kang to speak, he provided the amount of money that each illegal activity produced and, post laundering, how much would flow into the country's coffers and when. Once he finished, Kim Jong-un had the floor.

"I've recently negotiated a purchase of equipment for the Yongbyon Scientific Research Center," Kim Jong-un said, referring to the site which produced weapons-grade fissile material and housed a plutonium production reactor. "This was a feat that my advisors believed was impossible," he continued, patting himself on the back.

No one at the table believed anyone was stupid enough to tell the supreme leader that something was impossible. If they did, history showed that he killed them on the spot or sent them to a labor camp.

"Given the global sanctions prohibiting us and other emerging nuclear powers from purchasing anything that will expand or refine our programs, it took a year for me to out-negotiate Iran and secure this equipment."

Everyone at the table stood and applauded. With narcissism being one of his many personality disorders, Kim Jong-un smiled and shook his head in acknowledgment. Everyone continued to stand and clap until he signaled for them to sit.

"However," he continued, "if we cannot wire the payment one week before delivery, Iran will receive it. I assured the seller that our word was inviolate, and that we would make the payment on time." Kim Jong-un starred at Kang as he said this.

Kang squirmed in his chair.

"Talk to our money launderers and ensure they get the cash to our banks in time to make this payment. There can be no delays. Is that understood?"

"Understood," Kang replied. Judging from the expressions of everyone at the table, they knew that if there were a deficiency of cash which resulted in losing this equipment, there would correspondingly be a vacant seat at their next gathering.

When the meeting ended, Kang went outside to check his phone because, except through the hardened communications and data lines, the shielding within the bunker blocked any electronic signal from going into or out of the underground structure. Once his phone linked with the cell phone tower inside the compound, he saw he had a text message from Chao asking him to call. Kang did and, after their devices synced, Chao spoke.

"Jalwandi is dead. However, there's a complication." He explained that Gunter Wayan and his assistant were with Jalwandi at the time of his death, and there was a possibility he may have told them something.

"Have Desnam kill them," Kang said, referring to Paku Desnam, who'd dispatched Jalwandi.

"No one will know what happened to them," Chao promised and ended the call.

"Quite a shot," Dhani said, looking at the shattered window. The police photographer, the medical examiner, and the two detectives and forensics tech that Dhani brought were a whirl of activity around them.

"The shooter was, or still is, a military sniper."

"Given the marksmanship, that's a solid assumption," Dhani agreed. "I'll get a list of current and retired snipers from the military. Putting that aside for the moment, this would be a good time for you to tell me why you're here and what happened."

Wayan explained.

Dhani began asking a question but was interrupted when the coroner approached and told the captain that he was taking the body to the morgue. Once he left, Dhani asked his question.

"Was that your client?"

Wayan confirmed it was.

Dhani looked at the bottle of Macallan. "He had great taste in scotch. I should put this away before it disappears." He opened a door in the liquor cabinet and placed the Macallan inside.

"You gave me the mechanics of what happened, but you never said what you and your client discussed. Now that he's dead, there's no ethics barrier to telling me."

Wayan explained Jalwandi's involvement in organ harvesting and the funneling of money to North Korea but didn't mention The Organization, Sanadi, or Kang.

"Organ harvesting on this scale and North Korea's involvement are beyond my pay grade and the purview of my department. This needs to go to the Criminal Investigation Agency. Any idea where Jalwandi kept his records?"

"With me - at least some of them."

"What did he give you?"

"Five boxes. He said they were files, but I never looked inside."

"Where are the rest?"

"The rest?"

"I'm assuming there's more."

"I don't know."

"Tell me where the files are, and I'll send a couple of officers to get them."

"I can't do that. I keep all my historical records in the same space, and the boxes aren't marked. Having your people rummage through them negates the word private in private investigation."

"You could be there."

"Alongside the police! That visual wouldn't be conducive to my business."

"You have no business, Sam. From what I understand, this was your only client. You're unemployed."

"Self-employed. Nevertheless."

"Point taken," Dhani responded with a note of exasperation. "Where and when do you want to deliver the boxes to me?"

"At noon tomorrow in the parking lot of the Sacred Monkey Forest Sanctuary in Ubud."

"Why there?"

"I have my reasons."

"You're testing my patience. You should know that once I tell the Criminal Investigation Agency that the victim, who I now know is a criminal, gave you five boxes of files to store for him, they're going to want them immediately. They won't understand the delay. I'll run interference for you because we're friends, but if you don't show up tomorrow with them, they'll throw you inside a cell until you hand them over. They also might make you an accessory."

"I've worked with CIA before. Thanks for running interference."

After Wayan and Eka wrote an account of what occurred and handed it to Dhani, they left the house and walked to Eka's car.

"What was that all about?" Eka asked. "We don't have a records storage space unless you're referring to our small floor safe. And our client never gave us any boxes."

"Dhani knew Jalwandi."

"What?"

"He returned the Macallan to the exact spot from which Jalwandi removed it. There were eight doors in that cabinet - all the same size. How did he select the right one?"

"Thin. Do better than that," Eka said.

"When I told him I had five boxes, he asked where the rest were. How did he know there were more?"

"That might be tougher for him to explain."

"No matter. I have a way to find out what team he's playing for."

"That's why we're meeting him at the Sanctuary?"

Wayan nodded it was. "Speaking of tomorrow, any thoughts on where we can spend the night? It's not a good idea for either of us to go home. The sniper tried to kill us once; he may try again."

"Let me make a call."

The Bulgari Resort Bali is in Uluwatu and sits 492 feet above the sea. The ocean view villa, given to Wayan and Eka for the night, was one of eight along the cliff's edge. Each was within a walled compound replete with an infinity pool that appeared to merge with the Indian Ocean seamlessly. A magnificent garden of flowering trees and plants dominated three sides of their compound.

The villa was enormous, with Wayan commenting that the bathroom was nearly the size of his apartment. The sheer beauty of the resort and accommodations led him to remark that if there was a Garden of Eden on earth, this was it.

The Bulgari's manager, Anna Bello, was a close friend of Eka. An Italian transplant, the 44-year-old five-foot, eleven-inches tall beauty with stylish chestnut hair, met Eka one year ago through a mutual friend. Since then, the two head-turners socialized together - getting enough invitations for drinks to fill a small swimming pool. When Eka called and asked if they could get a room for the night, Anna was happy to help and comped their stay.

At seven the following day, they went to breakfast at Sangkar. No one seemed to be awake at that hour, and except for the staff, so the clifftop restaurant was empty. Eka selected an outside table. Both were famished and looked through the menu that was handed to them by the hostess. When the server came, Wayan ordered chicken martabak, a spicy omelet-pancake filled with eggs, green onions, and minced meat. The omelet-pancake was folded and cut into squares before being served. Eka ordered a fruit plate of papaya, lychee, salak, mangosteen, and rambutan. Both asked for coffee.

"You said you had a way to determine what team Dhani is on. How?" Eka asked once the server left.

"I'm not going to meet him in the parking lot at noon. Instead, we'll be in the hills above it. I want to see how he handles us not being there."

"That's not much of an answer. What do you expect to happen?"

"If he had a hand in killing Jalwandi or is part of The Organization, he'll leave and come after us, figuring the reason we're not there is that we suspect his involvement. He'll also believe that we know too much."

"Why didn't he kill us at Jalwandi's house after everyone left?" Eka asked.

"It would be too suspicious since everyone at the house saw us talking with him. Also, he wants the boxes."

"If he's involved, he might not wait until tomorrow. He might be looking for us now."

"Without question."

"But if he isn't involved with The Organization or isn't trying to get the boxes or kill us, what then?"

"I'll be full of remorse and apologize. As a police officer, he'll understand my caution."

"And you think how he handles us not showing up will give you an epiphany whether you can trust him?"

"Something will happen that shows us what side he's on."

Their coffee came. As both sipped the fresh brew, neither could have predicted what would happen and its unintended consequences.

CHAPTER 6

THE 27-ACRE SACRED Monkey Sanctuary in Ubud, whose only residents were approximately 1,000 long-tailed monkeys, was a hilly area densely packed with trees and bisected by a rocky stream. To the north and paralleling the stream was a meandering walking trail that ended in the village of Padangtegal.

Wayan and Eka arrived by taxi at 10 a.m. and staked out their position on a hill overlooking the parking lot. Using binoculars that they borrowed from the hotel, they watched the parking lot and waited. An hour later, a vehicle entered. Two men got out of the car. It didn't surprise Wayan to see that the driver was Riko Dhani because they'd agreed to meet here. However, when he saw his passenger was the man with the skull-like face, who got out of the vehicle carrying an elongated backpack, he shook his head in disappointment that his former partner had crossed over the line. After a brief conversation with Dhani, the sniper put on his backpack and began climbing the hill in back of him, which was to their left of Wayan and Eka.

"You were right when you said that something would happen which showed us what side Dhani's on," Eka said.

"He's using himself as bait. When we come out in the open to meet him, the sniper will take both of us out."

Wayan looked at the hill that the sniper was climbing but lost him in the dense concentration of trees.

"What should we do?" Eka asked.

"Get out of here. With a scope, it's only a matter of time until the sniper finds us. We'll walk down to the stream and use the footpath beside it to get to the village of Padangtengal."

"You know this area."

"My wife and I came here often. We can find a cab in the village and go back to the Bulgari." As Wayan and Eka took their first steps down the hill, a bullet hit the tree behind them. They didn't hear a gunshot, only the muted impact of the round hitting the tree. Wayan and Eka both dropped to the ground.

"You really should start carrying your gun," she said in an exasperated voice.

"It wouldn't do any good. Even if I could see the sniper, a handgun hasn't got the range or accuracy to hit him," Wayan replied defensively. "That exchange would be comparable to a demolition derby, where he's in a dump truck, and I'm in a compact car. Follow me." Wayan hunched down and led the way through the brush and down the hill.

Once on the footpath, they quick-stepped toward the village. It took 20 minutes to get there and another five to get to the taxi stand. There were no taxis.

"Done exercising?" Dhani said as he and the sniper, each holding a handgun, came from behind the taxi stand sign.

"How did you know we'd come here?" Wayan asked as he and Eka raised their hands.

"There are three ways to get to or leave the sanctuary. You can take a vehicle or go to one of two taxi stands - one is next to the parking lot, and the other is here. Since I didn't see either of your vehicles, where else could you have gone? When we got here, I flashed my badge and told the two taxis' that were here to leave."

"What now?"

"My associate, Paku Desnam, will frisk each of you. Then we'll take a trip."

The sniper did the pat-down while Dhani kept his gun trained on them. Once he'd finished, he pulled their arms behind their backs and tightened flex cuffs around their wrists.

"Into the car," Dhani ordered, pointing to his vehicle, which was ahead and to the right. Once they were in the back seat, Desnam flex cuffed their ankles.

"Where are we going?" Wayan asked.

"To give you a firsthand look at a facility your client established. After that, I'll explain what we do at the warehouse and ask each of you to make a donation. Sit back and relax; it will take an hour to get there."

The 25-mile drive to Bedugul, a village in the central highlands of Bali near the crater lakes, took almost exactly an hour. When they arrived at the warehouse, Desnam cut Wayan and Eka's leg ties and ushered them inside and up a set of stairs to the second floor. Pushed into a conference room, they were flex cuffed to a chair. Dhani was on his cell phone. When he finished, he approached Wayan.

"Do you know where you are?"

"Judging from your comment about making a donation, this is The Organization's organ harvesting center."

Dhani grinned at the mention of The Organization. "One of them. As we speak, surgery is taking place, so you'll have to wait. The room will be available in about 30 minutes. The unwilling donor is Jalwandi's attorney. After delivering the files that the general was hiding from us, we began questioning him. That took longer than expected because, besides Jalwandi, he has quite a few clients who may prove useful to us in the future. You didn't mention The Organization during our conversation at the house. What else are you hiding, Wayan?"

Eka interrupted. "Why are you doing this?" she asked.

"Don't be stupid - for the money, of course." Dhani was about to add to what he said when there was a knock on the door, and it was pushed open.

An Asian woman in her mid-50s walked into the conference room. She carried a plastic tray with two syringes, tourniquets, empty blood tubes with rubber caps, and other items associated with a lab tech. She went to Wayan first, drawing several tubes of blood, and then repeated the process with Eka. When she finished, she left without uttering a word.

"Compatibility testing," Dhani said, noticing Wayan and Eka's curiosity. "We'll put the results from your blood tests into our system. In a matter of minutes, we'll know which persons on our waiting list, either domestically or within Asia, have compatibility with your organs."

As Dhani spoke to his captives, Desnam sat in the conference room chair nearest the door and checked his phone messages.

"Tell me about your relationship with Jalwandi," Wayan asked.

"You still can't shake that natural sense of curiosity, even in the face of certain death. I admire that, Sam. Okay. Jalwandi and I met on the Tamala case, although not under the best circumstances since I wanted to convict someone in his command. However, he was an extraordinary judge of character, or I should say lack of, and called a few days later to ask if I wanted a part-time job that paid very well."

Dhani explained his job was to provide Jalwandi with the patrol routes for the department's drug interdiction vessels. In return, he received a monthly cash stipend equivalent to four months of detective's pay. In addition, every so often, Jalwandi provided him with information on illegal activities, all from The Organization's competitors, which Dhani told his superiors about, saying that it came from his snitches. This resulted in busting drug dealers, prostitution rings, and underground gambling establishments. Dhani's fame soared, and he quickly attained the rank of captain.

"Once I became captain, it was easier to deflect an investigation that might expose The Organization or me. Also, my part-time pay increased exponentially."

"But Jalwandi screwed everything up."

"And then some. He was going to expose everyone unless he received $100,000,000, later increased to $200,000,000. Can you believe it? He was dying. What could he do with the money?"

"Give you the middle finger," Wayan answered.

Dhani frowned. "Whatever the reason, it didn't sit well with his replacement. However, they didn't want to kill him until we got ahold of his files - the originals and copies. It would be disastrous if these fell into the wrong hands. Circumstances changed when his attorney offered us both."

"And now you don't have to worry about him telling anyone. That brings up the question - why didn't you kill me in the hospital?"

"I intended to. I had a syringe with a drug that would stop your heart and make it look like a heart attack."

"What stopped you?"

"There were too many people around. Although they left not long after Eka came, I couldn't very well ask her to wait in the hall and then tell the doctors you went into cardiac arrest. Too suspicious."

While they were speaking, an elderly five-foot, five-inch tall Asian woman had quietly entered the room through a door connected to her adjacent office. She was standing at the back, listening to their conversation. Desnam was the first to notice her and cleared his throat, which caused Dhani to look up.

"Let me introduce Aninda Basri, Amat Jalwandi's replacement," Dhani said.

The Asian lady appeared to be in her mid-60s. She wore no makeup and had salt and pepper hair pulled straight behind her neck and tied with a rubber band. Combined with her baggy clothing, which was devoid of style, she gave a clear impression that her appearance was not a priority.

"Here's trouble," Wayan whispered to Eka, no one else hearing the comment.

"Did Amat tell you about me?" she asked Wayan.

"He did, although not by name."

"He probably left out the fact that we were lovers. I was a colonel on his command staff and retired not long after him. It was purely physical, not emotional. After I replaced him in The Organization, I was going to let cancer take its course. I had no reason to question his loyalty. But then he bit the hand that fed him."

"And you sped up his demise," Wayan said.

"After getting what he held over us," she replied with a smile, revealing her teeth had yellowed.

"What a bitch," Eka said, transferring the center of attention to her.

"You and I will soon have a very personal conversation, sweetheart, while your friend is in surgery. Let me show you what I have in mind while I ask him a few questions. Tape their mouths and give me your knife," she said to Desnam.

The sniper took a roll of plastic wrapping tape from a cabinet behind him, tore off two strips, and taped Wayan and Eka's mouth. Reaching into his pocket, he removed a Frank Beltrame nine-inch stiletto switchblade and handed it to Basri.

"Where to begin?" Basri asked, thoughtfully tapping the blade of the knife to her lips. "Let's start with you," she said, putting the tip just above Wayan's knee and slitting the fabric to his hip. In the process, she pierced his skin, eliciting a guttural grunt from the private investigator. Pulling the slit apart to expose the upper portion of his leg, she touched the tip of the knife to his skin, pressed down slightly, and fileted away a section. Wayan, his mouth taped, bucked in his chair with muted screams of pain.

When she finished, she placed the bloody knife on the conference room table. "Did you tell anyone, except for your lovely assistant, what Major General Jalwandi told you?" Basri removed the tape covering Wayan's mouth.

Wayan took several gasps of air in quick succession and, breathing too hard to speak, shook his head no.

"Good. We're communicating. Did the general give you any papers, files, or electronic storage devices besides the five boxes?" she asked. Without waiting for a response, she placed the tape back over Wayan's mouth, grabbed the knife, and removed a smaller portion of skin.

Wayan again elicited a series of muffled screams, rocking his chair so hard that it would have fallen onto its side had not Desnam gripped the back of it.

Basri wiped the bloody blade on Wayan's shirt and again placed the knife on the conference room table as tears of pain ran down the private investigator's cheeks.

Eka, cuffed to her chair, was crying as she looked on.

Basri removed the tape covering Wayan's mouth. "Your answer," Basri said in a monotonal and unemotional voice.

"He didn't give me anything."

"You told the captain that he gave you five boxes of files. I want to know where they are."

"I said he didn't give me anything. I don't have any files," Wayan replied in gasps, the pain in his right leg excruciating. "I lied to Dhani."

"And now you're lying again. If you tell me what he gave you and where you hid it, I'll stop. I'll bring you downstairs to the doctor; he'll put an IV in your arm, and then no more pain. Otherwise, when we're through here, which I promise will be a harrowing experience, I'll tell him to forget about the anesthetic when he operates. It makes no difference to me."

Wayan was silent.

"No? Okay then." Basri placed the tape back over Wayan's mouth.

"Round three," she said, picking up the knife. "I only need your organs and not your limbs. Let's start with some simple amputations. I'll begin with the fingers on your right hand. If you're still uncooperative, I'll amputate those on your left. Still uncooperative? Your toes are next. You're dead either way, Wayan. Why endure the pain?"

As Basri bent down to place the blade over one of Wayan's fingers, two men burst into the room. Dressed in black, each had a Glock 21 with a silencer in their hand. While the taller of the two put a bullet into Desnam's head before the sniper could draw his weapon, the person beside him put two into Basri's cranium. Dhani, seeing this, raised his hands before the uninvited assailants made him their next casualty.

Picking up the switchblade that Basri dropped onto the floor, the shorter assailant cut Wayan and Eka loose while the other monitored Dhani.

"Tamala? I thought you were dead," Dhani stuttered as the army major pointed his gun at him while Wayan removed the handgun from the captain's shoulder holster.

"Kill him and let's get out of here," Captain Bakti Nabar said.

"Last words?" Tamala asked Dhani.

"You'll never get out of here alive," Dhani responded, the fear evident in his voice. "There are three highly trained security guards on patrol with orders to kill any intruder. No prisoners."

"Nice try. There were five guards on patrol, and given that they're dead, I'd say those orders are irrelevant."

"You forgot about those patrolling the interior."

"Dead. Two special forces officers are more than capable of neutralizing rent-a-cops."

The look on Dhani's face reflected helplessness and defeat. "I'll tell you anything you want; just let me live."

Wayan, who held Dhani's handgun in his left hand, grabbed Desnam's switchblade, which Nabar had placed on the conference room table after cutting him and Eka free. He calmly limped to where his former partner sat, put the barrel of the gun to the captain's forehead, and drove the knife through his right hand, pinning him to the table. Screams of pain radiated through the room.

"I have some questions of my own," Wayan said as he pulled a chair closer to him and sat down.

As Dhani began sobbing, Wayan ignored the pleading look that his former partner was giving him.

"Captain Nabar and I will do a thorough search of the warehouse. If he gives you any trouble, or has memory lapses, put a bullet in his kneecap," Tamala said before he and Nabar left the room.

"Eka, go outside," Wayan said.

"I want to stay."

"It could get messy."

"They were going to cut the organs from our bodies, Wayan. It doesn't get any messier than that."

"Good point."

CHAPTER 7

"THIS PLACE IS deserted, except for him," Tamala said, as he and Nabar shoved a middle-aged man dressed in green surgical scrubs into the conference room. The man had dark brown skin and was of average height and weight. "We also saw the surgery room."

"And?" Wayan asked.

"There's a body on a gurney. His eyes and internal organs are missing. Whoever was assisting this maggot probably left with them."

"Are you a doctor?" Wayan asked the man in scrubs.

The man remained silent until Tamala planted his fist in his gut, causing him to drop to his knees and cry out in pain.

"Answer the question," Tamala said as he pulled the man to his feet.

"Yes."

"How many people helped you kill the person on the gurney?"

"Two nurses assisted me in extracting the organs. The person who drew blood was one of them."

"Where did they go?"

"One went to Denpasar and the other to the Letkol Wisnu airstrip in Sumberkima, where private aircraft will transport the organs to the airport closest to the facility performing the transplant. Time is critical, as some organs deteriorate rapidly.

"Will the nurses return?"

"They were going to assist me with your surgeries."

"Not likely."

"Arrest me for all the good it will do. My employer assured me they would have any charge brought against me dismissed within a day," the doctor replied with a smirk. "I'm bulletproof."

"Really? Let's find out," Wayan said, raising his gun and putting two rounds into the doctor's heart.

"Feel better?" Tamala asked.

"Much."

"Why is he alive?" Nabar asked, looking at Dhani.

"My former partner told me all he knew about a host of subjects, including The Organization."

"Anything else you need from him?" Nabar asked, staring at Dhani.

"No."

"You're positive."

"Yes," Wayan confirmed.

Nabar put two bullets into Dhani's head. The inertia of those rounds would have thrown him out of the chair and backward onto the floor if not for the knife which anchored him to the conference room table.

"Don't waste your sympathy on him," Nabar said, looking at the shocked expression on Eka's face. "He's a disgrace to every officer who wears a badge. He needed his ticket punched."

"I wish I had the courage to do it," Eka responded.

"Make no mistake," Wayan said, "The Organization is going to come after us with everything they have, not only because we cost them a substantial amount of money by shutting this facility down, but also because we know too much. By us, I mean Eka and me because they won't know you helped us," Wayan said, pointing towards Tamala and Nabar.

"We need to hide," Eka said.

"Hide? I'm not hiding," Wayan replied. "I'm going after them."

"We can't possibly win."

"I need to because they will never stop coming after us. Even if we try to go off the grid, they'll still find us with their resources. We might as well select our graves beforehand."

"You're not going anywhere without me," Tamala corrected.

"Us," Nabar corrected.

"Eka and I have no choice but to fight back - you both have a choice."

"I looked at some of the files in the boxes that I was transporting," Tamala answered. "I'm in this fight."

"Why didn't you walk away and not get in the boat?"

"I wanted to confront the general."

"And say what?"

"Give the boxes to the authorities, or I will. Knowing you as I did, I didn't think you knew what was in the boxes. When we rendezvoused, I didn't believe you'd have a problem with that ultimatum once I told you what you were transporting."

"I wouldn't. By the way, why aren't you dead?"

"A combination of luck and the hypervigilence that comes from our training." Tamala explained that after stepping on the boat at the Jakarta marina, he looked at some files. Shocked by what he saw, he believed there might be more to this trip than he was told. He said he decided to inspect the vessel, finding a homing beacon installed next to the emergency locator beacon that was standard in most vessels. "The installation looked sloppy and hastily done," he continued. "Given the contents of the boxes and the extra beacon, I believed I was being set up. I didn't know how, but I wasn't about to find out. I changed my plans."

"Which is why you weren't on the boat when it exploded," Eka said.

"I took the boat out of the Jakarta marina in the event anyone was watching. However, instead of going to the rendezvous point, I stopped at the Cirebon marina, 180 miles to the southeast. There I found a boat captain for hire who would deliver the boxes for me."

"Did he look inside the boxes?"

"Yes, but not at the files. After seeing that all he was transporting was paper, he was fine."

"How'd you find him?"

"The marina manager gave me his name and vouched for him. His death weighs heavily on me. I thought that, if General Jalwandi were setting me up, he'd have plausible deniability."

"You didn't kill him, The Organization did," Wayan said.

"Yeah," Tamala replied, unconvinced.

"And you returned to base from Cirebon," Eka said.

"Yes. That's where I heard what happened."

"What did you do next?" Wayan asked.

"I was still going to confront Major General Jalwandi. Captain Nabar and I are friends and, after telling him what happened, he asked to come. We both took leave from the base and arrived at the general's house just as this piece of dirt," Tamala said, nodding towards Desnam's body, killed him.

Since we were both unarmed, and the killer was obviously a professional and not a rent-a-cop, there wasn't anything we could do. After he left, we saw you both exit the side gate. We followed you to the Bulgari and staked out the resort - which has only one way in or out. The next day, we trailed your taxi to the sanctuary but lost track of you in the dense undergrowth."

"How did you find us here?"

"We followed him," Nabar said, pointing to Dhani, "after we saw the sniper get into his car. "We trailed them to the village and watched them kidnap the both of you."

"But you have weapons now."

"We took them off the rent-a-cops we killed."

"This isn't a Hollywood movie where a scriptwriter guarantees a happy ending in the face of supposedly insurmountable odds. As I said, walk away."

"We're special forces. Risk is a part of our life," Tamala replied. "The files, along with what I saw downstairs, shows me that this entity you call The Organization is killing Indonesians - people I swore to protect. Listening to what the doctor said, I have no confidence the police or judicial system can solve this problem. We need to be the ones who dispense justice."

"Not everyone on the police force or in the judicial system is corrupt," Eka said.

"We don't have the time or the ability to separate the good from the bad."

"Do you go along with this?" Wayan asked Nabar.

"All the way."

"Then we give The Organization a bloody nose before we die."

"I'm setting my sights higher," Nabar responded. "I'm carrying three body bags with me. Those are for Sanadi, Chao, and Kang."

"What do you know about The Organization?" Tamala asked.

Wayan repeated what Jalwandi told him.

"Let's see if there's anything on these bodies to add to what we know," Tamala said.

While Wayan and Tamala searched the bodies, Nabar went to the operating room to retrieve the doctor's personal effects, since he was wearing scrubs that had no pockets. Eka searched Basri's office. Everyone placed what they retrieved on the conference room table.

The wallets contained only cash and credit cards. All the phones except one were old and didn't have either a fingerprint or facial recognition feature. Instead, they required a password for access. Dhani's newer phone had fingerprint access. Wayan, wiping the blood off the captain's finger, pressed it to the button.

As he was doing this, Nabar found a supply cabinet with various medical supplies. He put alcohol on what Basri had done to Wayan, eliciting several curses from the private investigator, and bandaged the wounds.

"What are you looking for?" Eka asked, seeing Wayan going through the contact list on Dhani's phone.

"Jalwandi mentioned that Sanadi, Chao, and Kang founded The Organization. They're in Dhani's contact list. Therefore, we know their physical location. Let's do the last thing they'd expect."

"Which is?" Eka asked.

"Going after them on their home turf."

"Hong Kong, China, and North Korea?" Tamala asked, not believing what he heard.

"I may rethink North Korea."

"Ballsy, but stupid."

The flames, which engulfed The Organization's organ extraction warehouse in Bedugul, began with Tamala and Nabar spreading alcohol from two 55-gallon drums throughout the building and igniting it. Seeing the flames from a distance, the returning nurses hightailed it out of there before the police cordoned off the area. The fire was visible for miles, and the warehouse collapsed before fire trucks arrived. Later ruled by the police and the fire department as arson trying to hide multiple homicides, they had no clue as to the perpetrators of the crimes.

As Wayan and Eka left Bedugul with the special forces officers, their discussion centered on how they could hurt The Organization, realizing they'd get the short end of the stick in a direct assault. All agreed their focus should be Sanadi because they weren't going to get to Chao in China or Kang in North Korea.

"Jalwandi said Sanadi is the lynchpin for their money-laundering operation," Wayan said. "If anyone has the information to put a dagger in the heart of this enterprise, it's him."

With everyone agreeing they should go to Hong Kong, Eka fronted the money and purchased four tickets. The next flight with seating left at 1:00 p.m. the following day. She next called her friend at the Bulgari to see if they could extend their stay, giving Wayan a thumbs up as she spoke.

On the way to the resort, they stopped at Eka's residence in Denpasar, where she packed a carry-on and retrieved her passport. With Tamala and Nabar's bags already in the trunk, their next stop was Wayan's apartment.

"It looks like someone ransacked the place," Tamala said when Wayan opened the door and saw that the contents of every drawer were thrown haphazardly on the floor.

Clearing debris on the right side of the kitchen floor next to one cabinet, Wayan pressed a release lever hidden in a floor molding joint. A square section of wooden floor released and popped up. Beneath it was a safe. Wayan entered the combination and pulled open the heavy square door, which measured 12 inches on each side. He removed his passport and $500 in US currency, leaving Amat Jalwandi's file, a Beretta 92FS handgun, and a box of ammunition inside.

"Give me your weapons," Wayan said to Tamala and Nabar. "I'll put them in the safe. You won't get them past airport security."

Tamala and Nabar handed him their handguns, which Wayan locked in the safe before latching the section of flooring over it. He then went into the bedroom, took some clothes and personal items off the floor, and placed them in a carry-on bag. Twenty minutes later, they arrived at the Bulgari.

CHAPTER 8

G ENERAL MIN KANG was about to have a panic attack after receiving a call from General Chao that a fire reduced their organ harvesting warehouse in Bedugul to twisted steel and charred rubble. Chao also said that he'd lost contact with Basri, Desnam, and Dhani - something he could not explain.

"I assume they're distancing themselves from the facility," Kang said, his statement sounding more like a pronouncement of hope than fact.

"I don't think so," Chao replied. "Their phones have GPS chips. My computer should be able to see where they are, but I'm not getting a signal. The most likely cause is that their phones are destroyed."

"When's the last time you heard from Dhani?"

"As Wayan and his assistant were being taken into the warehouse. I spoke with Basri when they were tied to chairs in the conference room, and she was going to question them."

"What if that pesky investigator killed them and burned down our facility?"

"Unarmed, with guards inside and outside the warehouse, his hands tied, and Desnam and Dhani next to him? That

77

seems highly improbable," Chao answered. "There's another explanation."

"If Basri died in the fire, we need to replace her quickly."

"That won't be difficult. There's always a line of those wanting to climb the ladder of monetary success."

Kang agreed.

"The bigger problem is determining what occurred at our facility to ensure it never happens again. The fire could be accidental, or a competitor is announcing they've entered our space."

"A competitor is an easy problem to rectify."

The conversation ended with Chao saying that he'd call if Basri or Dhani contacted him.

On the knife's edge for laundering the money needed for Kim Jong-un's purchase, Kang called Sanadi to understand the financial impact from the loss of the facility, hearing from him that Bedugul was a small part of their Indonesian operations and a ripple in The Organization's cash flow.

Although he knew Sanadi was right, this assurance did little to calm the inherently paranoid Kang because the supreme leader had zero tolerance for failure - the mental picture of those who'd been dragged from a meeting or shot where they sat vivid in his mind.

Following his conversations with Chao and Sanadi, Kang opened the center panel to a cabinet behind his desk and removed a bottle of soju, a colorless spirit made from rice and grains. The brand that he was drinking was 53 percent alcohol by volume. Filling a shot glass, he downed the fiery liquid in one gulp and repeated the process before returning the bottle to the cabinet. Calming down, he waited for Chao's call, hoping to hear that the warehouse fire was the only hiccup in their operations. That didn't happen - the following call from Chao making the first seem insignificant.

The five-hour Cathay Pacific flight to Hong Kong, a destination for which a visa wasn't necessary for Indonesians who stayed less than 30 days, landed on time. After clearing customs and immigration, they took a taxi to the Ritz. On the Kowloon side of Hong Kong Harbor, it comprised the top 17 floors of the 118-story International Commerce Center building or ICC as locals called it. The rest of the building was leased office space. The four shared one room, putting it on Eka's credit card. As she was filling out the registration form and getting their keycards, Wayan went to the concierge.

Their room on the 117th floor was spacious and had two double beds and a pull-out sofa. However, Eka asked housekeeping for a rollaway so that each person could have a separate bed. Once it arrived, they took the elevator up one floor to Ozone, the hotel's rooftop bar, which offered indoor and outside seating. They decided on an indoor table in the corner, which gave them both privacy and a spectacular view of the Hong Kong side of the harbor. No sooner were they seated than the server arrived. Although none of the four could speak Chinese, they knew enough English to communicate with the multi-lingual server. Wayan, Tamala, and Nabar ordered a Bintang beer. Eka, who preferred sweeter drinks, asked for a lemon drop martini. Once the server left, they began discussing how to get to Sanadi.

"His office, according to the address in Dhani's phone, is on the 101st floor of the ICC," Wayan said. "However, in speaking with the concierge, the office entrance and elevators are separate from the hotel."

"Let's see what we're dealing with," Eka said, accessing the hotel's guest internet service on her cell phone and bringing up the ICC's photo gallery. After scrolling to the business lobby photos, she placed the phone on their table so that everyone had a view.

"From what I see," Wayan said, moving the phone closer to him and looking at several of the photos, "there's a counter at the back of the lobby inside the office entrance. Behind the counter are two guards - at least that's what this photo shows." Wayan put his finger on the photo. "Six entry turnstiles are next to the counter, and beside each is a guard. With this level of security, we're not getting to the elevators unless someone puts our name on an access list."

Everyone agreed that getting past the guards would be a significant problem.

"Assuming we get past the guards and to Sanadi's office, we'll need weapons," Tamala said. "Sanadi will have security, and we may not get close enough to overpower them before they put a bullet in us or call for help. There's no easy way to escape when you're on the 101st floor. One call to the guards in the lobby, and we're done."

"I looked up Hong Kong's firearm restrictions before we left Bali," Wayan answered, "In Hong Kong, citizens can't have firearms unless they're military or police. Even then, they go through a strict permit process. We're not going to get a gun unless it's from the black market - and I don't think any of us know how to do that. However, we should assume that Sanadi's security detail is armed."

"What do you suggest?" Nabar asked.

"The best we can do is purchase tactical knives with foldable blades. At least we'll have a weapon."

"Bringing a knife to a gunfight. That should work," Tamala said in a voice that cast doubt on the viability of that strategy.

Wayan was about to say something but stopped until the server who delivered their drinks left.

"Do you have the Google Earth app?" Wayan asked Eka. Saying that she did, he gave her Sanadi's address.

"Maybe the best way to get to him is at his home," Wayan said.

"How far away from us does he live?" Nabar asked.

Tamala inputted both addresses into Google, which showed Sanadi's residence was approximately nine miles from them.

"It's closer than I thought," Nabar admitted.

"What can you find on the area in which he lives?" Wayan asked Tamala after looking at Eka, who shrugged and pointed to her phone, indicating she was waiting for Google Earth to show her the residence.

Tamala did another Google search, saying that the street Sanadi lived on was in an area called The Peak, which was short for Victoria Peak. "According to Google, it's the most expensive residential area in Hong Kong," he said as he laid his phone on the table so that everyone could read the narrative and see the image above it that showed a winding road through a high hill, or low mountain, depending on one's perspective, beside which were gates and the tops of residences hidden behind dense landscaping.

By this time, Eka brought up the picture of his residence, which gave an aerial view of Sanadi's compound. "He lives in a fortress," she said, looking at the image on her phone before putting it next to Tamala's so that everyone could see.

"It looks like there's a guardhouse just outside the gate to the property," Tamala said. "I can also see bollards, which are undoubtedly retractable, behind the gate."

"Our goal is to get enough information from Sanadi to destroy The Organization," Wayan said. "To do that, we'll need to get what's on the server. I don't think it will be at his home. That means taking him back to his office."

"He'll have a laptop or desktop at his residence. We can force him to access his server from there," Nabar said.

"Jalwandi told us that The Organization's computer system couldn't be accessed without a code from senior management. Sanadi obviously satisfies that requirement. Even using his computer, we may not be able to download the data to a laptop or storage device," Eka added. "The system, if it's as sophisticated as it seems, may not allow it."

"We have one shot at this," Wayan said. "Going after the server seems the safer bet."

"Which means we have to convince him to get us past the building's guards and into his office so we can take it," Tamala said, "not forgetting he'll have his security."

"I would expect that security would be significant and tight," Wayan said.

"The open question is, given what we know, how do we get close enough to Sanadi, at either his office or house, to grab him?" Nabar asked.

"We capture him between the two," Wayan answered.

"How?"

Wayan explained.

"We still have to take him to his office to get the server," Tamala said.

"With the right motivation, I'm counting on him getting us past the guards and his security."

"What's the right motivation?"

"He gets to live."

"That might work if we survive long enough to give him that option."

"Are you both in?"

Tamala and Nabar said that they were.

"When do we start?" Tamala asked.

"We'll do our recon tomorrow. The next day, our feet are in the fire."

"What do we do until then?"

"Have another round."

After two "last rounds," they went to the shopping center beneath the hotel, getting there a scant 20 minutes before the shops closed. Entering a large department store, each purchased a four-inch Al Mar Japan Eagle Classic folding knife and other items before guards began ushering everyone not in front of a register out of the store.

The flight, alcohol, and stress from what they went through and were planning to do took their toll, and everyone went to bed minutes after entering the room and slept straight through to the following morning. Eka was the first one up when, at 6 a.m., the alarm on her phone sounded. She got out of bed, hit the shower, and was ready within 30 minutes. Waking Wayan before leaving the room, she said she was on her way to Hertz. By the time she rented a car and returned to the hotel, it was 7:30 a.m. Wayan, Tamala, and Nabar were in front of the hotel when she pulled up. Each had a cup of coffee in their hand except for Wayan, who had two, handing one to Eka as he got in.

"Do you know where we're going?" Wayan asked after Eka took her first sip.

"I loaded Sanadi's home address before I left Hertz," she said, pushing the destination icon for Sanadi's home on the navigation system, the display in English. The route to Sanadi's residence appeared on the screen, indicating a distance of 8.6 miles.

Because they didn't know what time Sanadi left for work, and there was no place to park along the narrow road, they saw the residence as they passed it. Continuing to the observation platform, they got out of the vehicle and walked to the side that overlooked the road. Wayan, who saw from the Google image that the platform provided a view of the residential gates near the top of The Peak, looked through the binoculars purchased the night before. He focused on the gate to Sanadi's mansion because the high walls and dense landscaping blocked a view of the compound's interior.

At 9:30 a.m., an hour-and-a-half after he began his surveillance, the front gate opened and a Rolls-Royce Phantom, a $530,000 luxury car that weighed three tons, left the residence.

"That's a big vehicle," Wayan said, handing the binoculars to Tamala before the Phantom rounded a curve in the road and was out of sight. Wayan removed the phone from his pocket and looked up the various models of Rolls-Royce. As he scrolled through the photos, he pointed to one. "That's it," he said. Looking at its description, he saw a Phantom weighed nearly 6,000 pounds. "We're going to need a much heavier truck."

"You never said how we were going to get the truck," Tamala said. "We can't rent one because any damage to it would point back to the renter. We can't steal one because ..." Tamala stopped speaking when he saw the expression on Wayan's face.

"We're going to steal a truck?"

They repeated their surveillance that evening. It was dark when Sanadi returned home, and with the limited lighting surrounding his gate, they couldn't see much. All agreed their plan had a better chance of succeeding during daylight.

At 9:25 a.m. the following morning, Sanadi's Phantom exited his residence and turned left. The vehicle was traveling at 40 mph, which was fast for the winding two-lane road, although no other car was visible. As the direction of cars on Hong Kong streets was the same as in the United Kingdom, Wayan's truck was on the left side and hugging the hill. The 26-foot long five-ton vehicle they stole was going approximately 15 mph when the Phantom rounded a turn and came upon it. As the driver swerved right to avoid a collision, Wayan swung the truck in the same direction and pushed the lighter Phantom through the white knee-high wooden fence that bordered the road. The Rolls Royce went over the side.

The three-ton Phantom remained level as it tore through the thick vegetation at the top of the hill. However, as it descended and entered a denuded patch that sloped 45-degrees to the right, where the owner removed the dense vegetation because his wife wanted to plant something exotic he never heard of, which needed to be elevated for anyone to see it, the speed of the Phantom carried it across this denuded patch as if it was a launching ramp. The Phantom went airborne, landed on the equipment clearing the hill, and somersaulted until it came to rest in the pool area of the wealthy residents. Even though the vehicle's wheels were facing skyward, the sturdy roof did not buckle under the immense weight pressing on it.

Wayan, who brought the truck to a screeching halt and turned on its flashers, led the way over the shattered fence. It took several minutes for him and his team to arrive within 30 feet of the wreckage. That was as close as they could get and remain unseen. In front of them, three men stood beside the upside-down vehicle. Behind them was an older couple, who rushed back inside their house after seeing that the men had their guns drawn.

"I don't see Sanadi," Wayan said in a low voice.

That thought also occurred to the three men who, after looking around and seeing their employer wasn't standing near them, realized he was still in the vehicle. They returned their guns to their shoulder holsters. Two men reentered the Phantom through the non-existent side windows, seconds later pushing the body of a short, overweight man, dressed in a suit and tie, through the left side window opening. The guard who didn't enter the vehicle helped pull the limp body out and laid it flat on the pool deck. He was about to administer CPR; however, with Sanadi's eyes open in a vacant stare and his neck canted at an unnatural angle, indicating it was broken, it was obvious that he was dead.

Neither Wayan nor the other members of his team would ever learn that the reason for Sanadi's death was that he was the only one in the vehicle who didn't fasten his seat belt and shoulder harness. His failure to do so wasn't a one-time occurrence. He was a workaholic and always used the commute to access his email through the vehicle's Wi-Fi to and from the ICC.

Sanadi had his Rolls-Royce customized so that the rear passenger section was a mobile office. Part of this customization was a thick burled walnut panel that lowered from the rear of the front passenger seat and served as his desk. Another accommodation was a printer/scanner/copy machine hidden under the large twin armrests between the two passenger seats. However, in customizing the Phantom, he made one mistake - which cost him his life. To use the desk while wearing a seat belt and shoulder harness required the arm length of an NBA player. That wouldn't have been the case had the burled walnut panel been on extenders. Unfortunately, it wasn't. Sanadi was five feet, six inches tall and weighed 200 pounds. This meant that he had to sit on the edge of his seat to use the desk. Therefore, he never fastened his seat belt and shoulder harness.

"He's dead. Let's get out of here," Wayan said, seeing the guards standing over the body. He turned around and started back up the hill, with the others following.

Returning to the truck, Wayan put the pedal to the metal to get as far away from the crash site as possible before the police, which the older coupled undoubtedly called, arrived. Going back to Kowloon, they ditched the stolen vehicle several blocks from where Nabar hotwired it. After wiping down the surfaces they'd touched, they hailed a taxi and returned to their hotel room.

"I screwed up. I should have come up with a better plan," Wayan said upon entering the hotel room and throwing his keycard onto the desk. Sitting heavily on the couch, he took a deep breath and laid his head back.

"He was riding in a tank. How could he have died?" Eka asked. "No one else was injured."

"Your plan was solid. It was a freak accident," Tamala added. "If he survived the crash, Captain Nabar and I could have easily handled the security guards."

"But he didn't survive," Wayan said. "He's dead. While he was the lynchpin for money laundering and his death will hurt The Organization, they'll eventually find someone to replace him."

"What did you say?" Eka asked.

Wayan repeated it.

"The data is The Organization's carotid artery. Sanadi was their money-laundering genius. Everything he was doing should be on his server."

"We all agree. But how do we get at it?" Nabar asked. "We can't get to the elevator banks, much less their office?"

"Even if we get into his office, we can't access the data without Sanadi. We need a code for that, and I don't think Chao or Kang are going to give it to us," Tamala said.

"You're thinking micro. Think macro," Eka interrupted, eliciting a look of confusion from Tamala.

Wayan stared at Eka, working with her long enough to know her expression showed she knew how to do it. "Tell us how," Wayan said.

She did.

CHAPTER 9

BOTH MIN KANG and Hulin Chao had quantum encrypted cell phones which incorporated a particular type of SIM card. Given by the Chinese government to senior military officers, government officials, and influential politicians, these devices employed the laws of quantum physics to guarantee absolute security. Unlike traditional encryption, which relies on algorithms and can be cracked over time, any attempt to intercept a quantum encryption call will cause a physical change in the message, alerting the users to potential eavesdropping. This occurs because, as the call is initiated, quantum technology generates two keys. These verify the caller's identity and the call's information, ensuring intercept-free end-to-end encryption. Therefore, both Kang and Chao could speak freely without fear that either of their governments, or anyone else on the planet, could hear what they were saying. Chao obtained the devices, which could also receive calls from non-encrypted phones, from a shipment to the military, and distributed them within The Organization. They were visually identical to other cell phones.

Chao called to inform Kang of Sanadi's death, throwing the North Korean general into a full-scale panic attack. Chao tried to calm his partner, telling him that Sanadi's assistant, Melis Woo, could handle the situation until they found a replacement. However, his partner still viewed the demise of the financial guru as a catastrophic tsunami.

"Finding a replacement is easier said than done," Kang countered.

"General, we have no choice. I spoke with Woo. She seems competent and says there will be no delay in laundering our cash. Since Sanadi hired her, I assume she's competent, and that statement is accurate. The only change in our procedures is that, instead of Sanadi, we'll be the ones to issue her the access codes."

"If she can't launder the cash fast enough to give the supreme leader the money to make his purchase, I'll be dragged in front of a firing squad - if I'm lucky."

"Woo can handle it until I find a replacement. My people in Beijing will monitor her. Putting this aside, I have more unsettling news. Gunter Wayan and his assistant Eka Endah arrived in Hong Kong just before Sanadi's death. Fortunately, I placed their names in our immigration database with a "notify only" order after Dhani told me of their involvement with Jalwandi. They're staying at the Ritz."

"Then they're responsible for destroying our Indonesian warehouse and possibly killing Sanadi."

"They might have destroyed the warehouse and, since we still haven't heard from Basri, Dhani, or Desnam, somehow killing them. However, Sanadi died of a broken neck when his car went off the road. Woo was told of the accident, spoke with the guards, and called me. They said his car was going faster than it should and was too close to the edge of the road as it tried to pass a truck. The person responsible for his death is the driver, who's no longer an issue."

"Then why are Wayan and Endah in Hong Kong?" Kang asked. "I don't believe they're tourists. If they're here, they had something to do with his death. It should be easy for you to kill them since they're on your turf."

Although Chao agreed with Kang that they needed to die, he said their deaths should appear accidental so as not to initiate an investigation.

"Hong Kong isn't China - yet," Chao continued. "I might not be able to stop an investigation into the deaths of foreigners without creating suspicion as to my motivations."

"Can you kill them or not?"

"Accidents happen."

Eka's plan was to get into Sanadi's office, steal the server, and return to Indonesia. The four didn't plan to hand it to an Indonesian government official on their return because they'd committed a number of criminal acts to get it, including manslaughter and auto theft, with what they were about to do adding several more crimes to that list. Therefore, they could be deported and spend a decade or two in a Hong Kong jail. They agreed that anonymously sending the server, with a note explaining what was in it, seemed the better way to go.

Their first hurdle was getting past the guards at the security desk in the ICC's business lobby. Eka offered a unique way of doing this by, as she said, exploiting their expectations. After explaining what that meant, everyone agreed her plan could work. However, the consensus was that all of them couldn't go because four people seeking access to the same office, which probably didn't have many visitors, would be suspicious. They decided that Wayan and Tamala should be the ones to get the server.

After getting the name of a uniform shop and an electronics merchandiser from the concierge, Wayan and Tamala left the hotel for a section of southern Kowloon that locals referred to as TST, short for Tsim Sha Tsui. Once they left, Eka extended their hotel stay for another day before she and Nabar went to the office supply store and the FedEx office in the shopping center below it. They returned 30 minutes later.

It was ten minutes to noon when Wayan and Tamala returned.

"How did it go?" Eka asked.

"Have you ever tried to get a FedEx uniform in Hong Kong for someone six feet, five inches tall?" Wayan said, pointing to Tamala. "He's a tree compared to the locals. The good news is that I wasn't at my credit limit on one of my cards and offered to pay three times the going rate for a tailored uniform if they'd get it done within an hour. While everyone was sewing, we went to an electronics merchandiser down the street and bought this," Wayan said, removing a barcode gun from the plastic bag that he was carrying. "My card is once again maxed out."

"Put the uniforms on," Eka said.

Wayan and Tamala stripped down and changed.

"Perfect," Nabar remarked.

"How did you do?" Wayan asked him.

"We picked up blank airbills and boxes from the FedEx office and bought copy paper at the office supply store."

"It's already noon," he said, looking at the clock in their room, "we'd better get moving."

The plan called for them to approach the lobby guards around 12:30 p.m. - a time that Eka believed many people from the 101 floors of business offices would leave the building for lunch, and food delivery couriers would be arriving. They divided up the remaining tasks. Nabar and Tamala would assemble eight FedEx boxes and put enough paper inside to give them weight. Eka and Wayan would fill out the airbills, using as the sender the address of the electronics merchandiser on the receipt Wayan was provided.

It was 12:20 p.m. when Wayan and Tamala left the hotel, each carrying four FedEx boxes. Neither had a FedEx ID, nor would the building's security guards see a vehicle bearing the company's logo when they looked through the expansive lobby windows. Since there was no way to overcome these obstacles in such a short amount of time, they know they just had to go for it.

As expected, there were long lines of food delivery people and others waiting in front of the two guards at the security desk. Each person needed a pass to proceed through the turnstiles and access the elevators. Wayan chose the line on his left because the expression on that guard's face showed he was more frazzled than the guard next to him, although it was close.

As the line moved forward, and although they couldn't understand Mandarin or Cantonese, it appeared the guard asked each person who they wanted to see and held out his hand for their identification. At least that was their interpretation. After checking his computer, he would issue a paper pass containing a barcode. When the recipient held it over the optical reader, the turnstile released, with the guard standing beside it watching the process.

When it was Wayan and Tamala's turn, the guard looked at their uniforms and the boxes each held. Although the rule was that everyone was required to have an access pass, it didn't apply to parcel delivery services because those within the building seldom knew when packages would arrive. Therefore, the guard asked what they were doing in line and if they were new because they should have gone directly to the turnstile. Neither Wayan nor Tamala understood Chinese, but they saw that the guard was pointing to the turnstile nearest him and speaking to the guard beside it who beckoned them over. The guard, using his ID card, released the turnstile and let them through.

They found the elevator bank for the top floors, entering an elegantly paneled enclosure lined with dark, highly polished wood. Wayan pushed the button for the 101st floor and, after a 15-second delay, the doors closed. They began their ascent at an impressive rate of speed, with Tamala's ears popping halfway to their destination, given that atmospheric pressure decreased with altitude causing tension inside the ear to increase. Wayan had an expression of pain on his face as he opened and closed his mouth, coughed, and cleared his throat.

"Do you have a problem with your ears?" Tamala asked, noticing what he was going through.

"They're killing me."

"You need to equalize the pressure. A pilot once told me to take a breath, close my mouth, hold my nose, and gently exhale. If you do this, the inner ear will open."

Wayan tried it, and his earache immediately disappeared.

"Thanks. I thought my head was going to explode."

Twenty seconds later, the elevator doors opened, and they exited onto a thick brown carpet that looked better suited for a Beverly Hills mansion than an office building corridor.

"Suite 10104," Wayan said, looking at the address on the airbill - which they'd previously gotten from Dhani's phone.

They found the office around the corner to their left. The door to the suite was the same dark wood that paneled the elevator. Next to the door was a buzzer, an intercom with a recessed camera incorporated into it, and an RFID reader. Wayan pressed the buzzer, and ten seconds later, a metallic voice came through the box.

"Yes?"

"FedEx," Wayan said in English, which was the business language of Hong Kong.

"Just a moment," a woman responded.

The door lock released. Wayan and Tamala entered the 2000-square-foot space. If they had time, they would have seen that to the left of the central corridor were a conference room, small kitchen, and bathroom. To the right were three offices and the server room. However, they didn't notice any of this because their focus was on the four guards pointing handguns at them. A woman, with a bemused smile on her face, stepped from behind them.

"Greetings, gentlemen, my name is Melis Woo," the five feet, four inches tall woman said in the voice they'd heard on the intercom. She appeared to be in her mid-40s, had black hair and light brown eyes, and a decent figure. She was wearing a dark blue business suit that looked expensive. "General Chao said you might visit me following the death of Mr. Sanadi. However, Mr. Wayan, I expected your assistant Eka Endah would accompany you. He sent me both of your passport photographs from immigration control at the airport. It appears there are more of you than we thought. No matter. Get what they're carrying and frisk them," she said to the guards.

They were patted down, and their pockets emptied.

Woo ordered that they be taken to the conference room and watched as the guards laid the items from Wayan and Tamala's pockets, along with the FedEx boxes, on the conference room table.

"Let's see what you were bringing me," Woo said, opening the FedEx boxes and seeing that they contained blank sheets of paper.

"These must have been heavy to carry. Good, you'll need to be strong for what I have planned." She turned and told one of the guards to get a roll of duct tape. When he returned, she had him bind Wayan and Tamala tightly to their chairs.

Woo opened one of the passports and removed the driver's license from the wallet beside it. "Gunter Wayan, age 33, and living in Bali. And who is our mystery guest?" she asked, opening the second passport and removing the driver's license from the wallet. "Langit Tamala, age 30, and living in Jakarta. What's this?" she asked, seeing a military ID, which had been behind the driver's license. "You're an Indonesian army major. How interesting. Watch them," she said to no one in particular, "while I make a phone call."

Five minutes later, she returned carrying a plastic toolbox in one hand and a silenced Heckler & Koch MP5 submachine gun in the other. "I'm going to question them while you four go to the hotel to kill his assistant, Eka Endah, and anyone who is with her," Woo said, handing a guard the room key, which she took off the table. "Do it quietly and make it look like she dropped her curling iron in the bathtub or tripped and hit her head. It's got to appear to be an accident."

As they waited for Wayan and Tamala to return, Nabar grew increasingly restless and told Eka that he felt useless sitting in their hotel room. A special operations soldier, he expected to be the tip of the spear in any operation and not waiting for an after-action report. "I'm going downstairs for a smoke," he said.

"I didn't know you were a smoker."

"Off and on. If things get tight and I'm not on deployment, I light up. In the field, I chew."

Eka gave him a face showing that she was not a fan of that habit.

"I know."

Taking her keycard, he went downstairs to a shop near the reception desk and bought a pack of cigarettes, going outside to light up. He was halfway through his first cancer stick when he saw the four guards, two of whom he had seen with Sanadi, striding towards the hotel entrance. Each seemed tense as they entered the building. "Eka," he said to himself.

Throwing his cigarette into the bushes, he took out his phone but quickly put it back in his pocket when he realized he didn't have her number or that of the Ritz. Running into the hotel, he followed the men into the elevator. Two were to his right, one directly in front, and one to his left. The man to his left pressed the number for their floor.

After the door closed, they began their 80-second ascent to the 117th floor. Out of the corner of his eye, he saw the man to his right elbow the person beside him.

"Where are you from?" the man asked in broken English. Although his question tried to portray that his inquiry was casual, his tone indicated otherwise."

"Asia."

"I meant what country."

"Singapore."

"Funny, you look Indonesian."

"What about you?" Nabar asked

"I'm local," the man answered as he unbuttoned his jacket. The other men, seeing this, did the same.

On paper, the ensuing fight was a mismatch. There were four guards, and the skinniest outweighed Nabar by 75 pounds. Also, each carried a handgun in a shoulder holster. However, there is no such thing as a fair fight in combat, nor does everyone wait until both sides agree they're ready. Nabar struck first, kicking the guard standing in front of him in the balls with the toe of his boot. As he screamed and collapsed onto the elevator floor, he punched the person to his right, the one who had been asking questions, in the throat. This caused him to fall to his knees, gasping for breath. Both actions occurred in a little over a second. As the two remaining men reached for their weapons, Nabar kicked the last standing guard to his right in the left knee. Although it didn't break, it was a showstopper. The man fell on top of the first guard, who was panting because his throat had swelled to where he couldn't take a deep breath. His last adversary had his gun out of his holster and turned it towards him. The special forces operator grabbed his wrist before he could pull the trigger and violently twisted it until he released the weapon. Once out of his hand, Nabar punched him in the face and broke his nose. Disarming the four guards, he held a gun on them until the elevator doors opened, directing them to his room and having one of them knock on the door.

Opening it, Eka was surprised to see four moaning men standing in front of her - all having difficulty standing, and one bleeding from his nose.

"Go inside and sit on the floor with your fingers interlaced behind your head," Nabar ordered.

The men complied, and Eka put a "Do Not Disturb" card on the door handle. He explained what happened.

"Apparently, they believed that, because I looked Indonesian, I was a threat."

"These are big men. How did you overpower them?"

"I'm the martial arts instructor for the Kopassus, the army's special forces group. In a confined space with the element of surprise, and with my skill level, the outcome was never in doubt."

"What about the elevator and hallway cameras."

"I saw neither. I found this when I searched them," Nabar said, handing her the keycard to their room.

"They have Wayan and Tamala,"

"It looks like it."

"What do we do?"

"Rescue them, of course."

CHAPTER 10

ENERAL HULIN CHAO'S call from Melis Woo saying that she captured Wayan did not surprise him. He believed the private investigator was in Hong Kong to look into Sanadi, and by extension, The Organization. What better place to start than his office? The surprise was that he had an Indonesian special forces officer with him, which begged the question of who else he told about The Organization. Woo would hopefully find out.

He concurred with her decision to kill the assistant, make it look like an accident, and leave her in the room so that housekeeping would find her. She was duplicative. Wayan and Tamala would give him everything she knew. Making her death look accidental meant he didn't have to worry about a murder investigation. That might involve Hong Kong investigators speaking with an unknown sphere of people connected with Wayan and Tamala. Who knew where that could lead?

He realized that there was no simple way out of his situation; having three accidental deaths on the same day involving parties who knew each other strained the bounds of credulity, especially when they were in different locations. Therefore, knowing that the discovery of Wayan and Tamala's bodies would trigger a murder investigation no matter what the cause, Chao decided to forget about making their deaths appear accidental. He'd send someone to get rid of the bodies and let the Hong Kong police focus on finding two missing persons - if anyone even filed a report.

"Forget about making Wayan and Tamala's deaths look accidental. Once you've gotten everything they know, kill them and call me," Chao said, initiating his new strategy. "Call me once they're dead, and I'll send a team to get the bodies. I know this is new to you. If you have trouble murdering them, the men that I'm sending will do it."

"I'll try to keep their blood off the furniture."

Chao seemed pleased with that remark and ended by telling Woo that he was happy with her performance and that her offshore account would soon receive a wire reflecting this appreciation.

Having just sent the guards to the Ritz, Melis Woo removed a pack of Marlboro Lights and a lighter from her pocket, tapped a cigarette from the pack, and lit it. With the cigarette dangling from her lips, she opened the toolbox and removed a six-inch knife, wire cutters, and a pair of needle-nose pliers.

"Here's the story. My boss ordered me to torture both of you to find out what you know about The Organization, who you told, and why you're here. Afterward, I'll put one or two bullets into your heads. My suggestion is to make this experience as short as possible and tell me what I want to know. Don't make me torture you any longer than necessary. As I've never tortured anyone because my specialty is computers and finance, I took this toolbox from the kitchen.

It contains several items that look like they can inflict a great deal of pain."

"I don't suppose there's a possibility of you dying of lung cancer before we start?" Wayan asked.

"My genetics aren't in your favor. My grandmother is in her 90s and still smokes. I only smoke in stressful situations."

"Can we have a cigarette?"

Woo thought for a second before answering. "Absolutely. First, I need to do something to prevent our neighbors from hearing your screams." Tearing two strips of duct tape from the roll the guards left on the table, she placed them over Wayan and Tamala's mouths, "Now, let me give you your cigarettes."

When establishing The Organization - Kang, Chao, and Sanadi were careful to only communicate through their quantum phones. Therefore, they assumed every conversation between them was unmonitorable. Upon Sanadi's death, a guard gave his cell phone to Woo, who placed it on her desk next to hers.

While Chao's calls to Woo went to Sanadi's encrypted device, which she promptly answered, her subsequent call to him was from her personal cell phone - something Chao never knew because his phone could receive both encrypted and unencrypted calls. Woo didn't know to use her late employer's phone because neither Sanadi nor Chao told her their devices had encryption capability. However, Chao assumed she knew about the encryption. Therefore, not knowing there was a difference, she used her personal phone instead of Sanadi's when she called him. Adding to the confusion was that Woo set up her phone so that it didn't reveal her number, with the warning "No Caller ID" appearing on the recipient's phone, the same description generated by Chao, Sanadi, and Kang's encrypted devices. Chao thought she was on Sanadi's phone. Instead, she was speaking to him in the clear.

Everyone in China understood that the Ministry of State Security, or MSS, intercepted domestic and international conversations because it handled foreign intelligence, counterintelligence, and political security. Woo's call to Chao began its electronic journey by connecting with a cellular tower near her office, went through the local Hong Kong telecom exchange, and passed through several towers and exchanges on its way to Beijing. Once connected, a sophisticated MSS algorithm filter within a mainland China exchange recorded and analyzed the call to determine if illegal or subversive activities were discussed. If the computer analysis decided this was possible, the recorded conversation went to the MSS for manual review. In contrast, if the call was benign, the recording was deleted.

A combination of words such as *kill her, kill both,* and *remove the bodies,* when used in context with what else was said, got the attention of the MSS algorithm, and the Chao-Woo conversation was sent for manual review. Also, because it included a discussion about an impending crime, a red flag was attached to the recording, meaning that it was a priority, and the computer pulled whatever electronic records existed on the caller and the recipient. In China, that essentially meant one's life history. Moreover, when the computer showed that one phone belonged to the military, the recording and electronic records were automatically diverted from the MSS to army intelligence.

The army officer who got the MSS recording received his commission eleven months ago. He craved some measure of excitement in his life, short of being shot at, and was bored out of his mind reviewing these types of recordings because he quickly discovered that military jargon was replete with descriptive words and phrases involving mayhem. Therefore, he deemed his job as a career killer because he was the very definition of a dispensable pencil pusher.

After listening to the discussion between Woo and Chao, he believed an investigation was merited. However, there was a complication. One party was a four-star general. That was a double-edged sword. If he banged the drum and pushed through the paperwork to begin a formal investigation of General Chao, and if there were something there, he'd be promoted from pencil pusher to a more robust job. However, if that investigation determined this was worthless chatter, or exposed a sensitive operation, then his judgment would be called into question, and the four-star would put his boot up his ass. That meant a transfer to a frontier post and a thick black "do not promote" mark on his record - a common scenario, he'd been told, for someone who pissed off the military equivalent of God. Therefore, the officer kicked the can down the road, forwarding the recording and attached electronic file to his boss, figuring he would still get credit if he uncovered an impropriety but wouldn't be risking his career.

When his boss received the information, he came to the same conclusion as the newly commissioned officer and passed the file and recording to his boss. This thought process continued, the recording and file working their way up the chain of command. The response of every officer in the military hierarchy was the same - except for one.

Captain Bakti Nabar and Eka Endah entered the business lobby of the ICC building. Using the access cards that they'd taken from the wallets of the guards, who were tied up in their room with a DND sign hanging from the door handle, they passed their cards over the electronic reader and went through the turnstile. After entering the elevator car, they pressed the button for the 101st floor and waited. Ten seconds later, the doors closed, and it began its ascent.

"Do you think," Eka asked, pointing to the rectangular plastic card in his hand, "that will get us into Sanadi's office?"

"If not, I'll try and kick the door in."

"Try?"

"It only works about 50 percent of the time because some doors are designed to prevent that type of incursion."

"And the other 50 percent?"

"I dive to the ground because the element of surprise is gone, and there's usually a bunch of bullets coming at me."

The look on Eka's face reflected what she'd heard wasn't reassuring. She refrained from asking Nabar any more questions.

Arriving on the 101st floor, they made their way to suite 10104. The look of concern on Eka's face visibly lessened when she saw an RFID reader next to the door.

"We're in luck," Nabar whispered, removing the two handguns that he'd taken from the guards and hid under his jacket. He handed one to Eka. "Are you ready?"

Eka, who was standing behind the special forces officer, whispered that she was. Nabar held the RFID card over the reader and the door lock released. As they stepped inside, they heard a series of grunts coming from a room ahead and to their left. The look on Eka's face was one of horror, realizing it was the same sound that she heard Wayan make as Basri was torturing him, his screams muffled because his mouth was taped shut.

"It's about time," a woman's voice yelled from the room in question. "Any trouble killing the bitch?"

Nabar, holding the gun in the ready position with his arms extended, led the way into the conference room. In front of them, a middle-aged woman took a puff off a cigarette. Wayan and Tamala, bound with duct tape to conference room chairs, had their clothing pulled back, exposing their arms and legs, which bore multiple circular burn marks. Their torturer, who had a submachine gun on the conference room table within easy reach, and various maintenance tools beside it, was so preoccupied with her interrogation that she never turned around. Wayan and Tamala were looking at their wounds. Nabar stepped forward and struck Woo in the back of her head with the butt of his gun, and she collapsed unconscious onto the floor.

"Cut them loose," Nabar said, taking the knife off the conference room table and handing it to Eka. "I'll secure this woman."

After picking Woo up and putting her in a conference room chair, Nabar took what remained of the duct tape and secured her with it. As he was doing this, Eka cut Wayan and Tamala free.

"We need to put something on those," she said, looking at their burns.

"You're right - these hurt like hell," Wayan said. "Once we're out of here, you and Captain Nabar need to explain over drinks how you were able to rescue us. I'm buying."

"Damn straight you're buying," Nabar said, overhearing the conversation.

Tamala was silent as he frisked Woo while Nabar was securing her to the chair. When he finished, he placed the cell phone that he'd taken from her pocket on the conference room table.

"Want me to wake her up?" Nabar asked.

"Not yet," Wayan replied. "Let's search the office. Eka, can you watch her while we do that?"

Saying she would, she sat in a chair and pointed her handgun at Woo.

They started on the right side of the central corridor, with the room closest to the entry door. Inside that office, they found a Dell desktop computer. The screen was black, and the desk contained standard office supplies but no personal items. There were no photographs or pictures in the office. Their impression was that this was a guest office. However, that changed when they found a Burberry raincoat and matching hat on a hook behind the door.

"This must be Melis Woo's office," Tamala said.

"Which means this is her computer," Wayan responded, sitting in the tufted white fabric chair in front of it. As he moved the mouse, the screen changed from black to light blue, and a pop-up box appeared requesting a decryption key.

They entered the office next door, which was significantly larger than the one they left. There was an empty credenza behind the desk and a couch against the far wall. As with the office they'd left, there were no personal effects visible, and a Dell desktop computer and keyboard were the only other items on the desk. Wayan turned it on, and a logon screen appeared.

"This might be Sanadi's office," Wayan said.

"I've never seen such a sterile work environment."

"They don't make it easy to look under the covers; I'll give them that."

The last office appeared to be unused as there was no computer on the desk and, as with the other two offices, no personal items were visible.

The next space was the server room. It was small, cold, and had a black metal rack attached to the back wall. The rack contained the server, which was thirteen inches wide, ten inches deep, and one inch high. The equipment on the shelf beneath it was some type of electronics component that was eight inches to a side and two inches in height. Below these were two backup batteries.

"We'll come back and get these before we leave," Wayan said.

They left the server room, walked to the other side of the corridor, and entered the kitchen, which was to the right of the conference room. Resting on the white tile counter, next to a full-size refrigerator, was a microwave, Keurig brewing system, a roll of white paper towels, six empty coffee cups, and other accessories found in an office kitchen. The room to the kitchen's right was the bathroom, which was unremarkable except for the first aid kit attached to the wall. Wayan opened it. Inside were gauze pads, cotton balls, adhesive bandages, cohesive wraps, Neosporin, and related medical supplies. Tamala took it to the conference room, where he and Wayan attended to their burns, and Wayan changed the dressing on the wounds inflicted earlier by Aninda Basri.

"I think it's time we talk to Melis Woo," Wayan said, rolling a conference room chair in front of her and sitting down.

Woo was still unconscious, with her head slumped forward. Wayan tapped the side of her face until she regained consciousness. As her eyes opened, she blinked several times and scanned the room with a confused look.

"Remember me? I think it's time you answered some questions," Wayan said, looking at the person who tortured him and Tamala and ordered Eka killed.

Woo's response was to spit at the private investigator, although her aim was off and, instead of hitting his face, the spit landed on his right shoulder.

Wayan was unflustered as he got up and took a cigarette from the pack on the conference table. After lighting it, he took off the floor the strip of duct tape previously over his mouth and put it tightly over Woo's. Kneeling, he removed her Valentino sandals and set them to the side.

"As I said, I have some questions. Let's start with what do you do for The Organization." Wayan removed the tape and waited for her answer. This time, she began screaming at him in Chinese.

Calmly returning the duct tape to her mouth, Wayan touched the tip of the cigarette to the top of her right foot. Woo bucked violently in her chair while Tamala held its back so that it wouldn't tip over. As tears streamed down his former inquisitor's cheeks, he unemotionally relit his cigarette. "I can keep this up all day. If I need more cigarettes, there's a sundry shop in the hotel lobby," Wayan said as he knelt in front of her.

Woo rapidly shook her head from side to side, indicating that she had enough. Wayan removed the duct tape from her mouth.

"General Chao will kill me if I tell you anything. You don't know what he's capable of."

"I don't care. Answer my question, or that scar on your foot is going to have a twin."

Woo involuntarily scrunched the toes on the assaulted foot.

"This is The Organization's clearinghouse. Mr. Sanadi and I launder cash and ensure that, by a multitude of financial routes, it gets to North Korea after taking our cut."

"Explain what launder means," Nabar, who was standing to Wayan's left, said.

"Making the money appear to have come from a legal source. It's a three-step process. The first is putting the money into a legitimate financial institution. That isn't easy because banks must report large cash deposits or what's referred to as high-value transactions. Getting too complicated?" Woo asked in a tone that seemed to imply that Nabar didn't have the cerebral horsepower to understand.

"Keep going."

Woo glanced at her foot and decided that giving her captors grief was decidedly not in her best interest. She ratcheted down her antagonism a notch or two and explained that the second step was layering, or sending this money through various financial transactions to change its form, making it more difficult to track. "This involves bank-to-bank transfers, which funnels money to different accounts in different names and different countries. It also involves changing currencies and purchasing high-value items to change the form of the asset," she explained.

"And step three?" Tamala asked.

"Integration. The money enters the economy in a legitimate-looking form, appearing to come from an unquestionable transaction. For example, a bank transfer that supposedly came from the sale of a yacht, a receipt of cash from an investor, and so forth. At this point, the money in the financial institution is legal."

"But an audit would uncover these illegalities," Eka said.

"Not unless someone is stupid enough to keep records from the layering process. Getting caught with this documentation is catastrophic and exposes the laundering process. Without it, a discovery audit and subsequent prosecution are nearly impossible."

"Did Sanadi put all of this together?" Wayan asked.

"Let's say this office assembled the small army of attorneys, intermediaries, and secondary accountants to enact the many processes to launder the nearly $2 billion we clean each month. Sanadi and I directed this operation."

"What do you mean by direct?" Nabar asked.

"Think of a music conductor. Does he play an instrument? No. But he knows every note in a piece and how to integrate the instruments in the orchestra to get the desired outcome and the applause."

"You sound proud of this illegal enterprise," Eka said.

"I am. Very."

"I have another question," Nabar said. "You said billions. How can you layer billions? Isn't a bank going to question the source of hundreds of millions of dollars that are deposited into it?"

"Of course. But they won't see hundreds of millions of dollars. Instead, they see thousands - which is an amount that's too small to raise suspicions. The financial infrastructure laundering The Organization's money involves over 2,500 bank accounts. These are in a multitude of names in several hundred banks in 30 countries. We keep the transactions under $10,000 in cash so that we're below the tripwire for financial reports. Again, we have numerous lawyers on retainers who set up these accounts. They don't know what they're for, although some might suspect. They only know that they're establishing one or more bank accounts for their client's thriving business. They're also paid to ensure that the tax filings, annual reports, and so on for the company are current."

"The Organization must have purchased quite a few enterprises to wash this cash," Wayan said.

"Bravo. One of you isn't a caveperson. Can you give me an example of the best enterprises to clean this quantity of cash?"

"Since I assume that most of the cash comes from outside Hong Kong, the import and export of commodities is the obvious choice. An example. An importer buys goods for an existing order, let's say Colombian coffee. You're not price sensitive since you're washing money. You sell the coffee to whoever gave you the contract, such as a large chain store or broker in another country. When the beans arrive, you receive clean money from whoever purchased the coffee. The process is the same for other transactions besides commodities."

"You're smart."

"Won't some government eventually notice the large number of wired money transactions, even though they're small, and become suspicious?" Nabar asked.

"Hundreds of thousands of global wires, totaling trillions of dollars, occur daily. A needle in a haystack would be substantially easier to find, even using sophisticated algorithms. As you said, these are small dollar amounts."

"Which brings us to the server," Wayan said. "We need the digital access code to your computer so we can access its data."

"I don't have it. It's an RSA system."

"RSA?" Tamala asked.

"It's too complicated to explain, and you wouldn't understand it anyway. Google the letters and do your best to comprehend the explanation. The bottom line: I'm only given the digital decryption key to the folders I need, and it's only valid for a specified amount of time. General's Chao and Kang are the only persons who have the master decryption key."

"Didn't Sanadi have the master key?" Nabar asked.

"If the key is in the same location as the clearinghouse, what's the point? Someone like you could put a gun to our heads, just as you're doing now."

"You must know how to get around the decryption key," Tamala said.

"You'd need America's NSA to do that."

"We'll take the server with us and get someone to crack it," Wayan said.

"Intelligence agencies in America, China, Russia, Great Britain, and possibly several other countries have the sophistication to do it, although it will take time. I doubt Indonesia has that capability. Take the server, but it won't get you anywhere."

"Getting past the server, you must have written down the names of the companies and their banks," Tamala said.

"Haven't you been listening? I said there were over 2,500 bank accounts in 30 countries. Washing money is dynamic. Over time, bank accounts are opened and closed, and countries are added and subtracted. Therefore, I require my computer to launder our cash. That means an access code. Also, if Sanadi, Chao, or Kang even suspected I wrote anything down, they would kill me."

Woo's phone chirped.

"Since you can't help us, is there any reason I shouldn't kill you?" Wayan asked.

"I was about to mention one. Did you hear my phone chirping?"

Everyone acknowledged they did since it was on the conference room table.

"When I captured the two of you," Woo said, looking at Wayan and Tamala, "I called General Chao. He's a micromanager and not a patient man. The chirp you heard indicates that he's the caller. That was the third chirp. Our internal protocol dictates that if three consecutive calls from him or Kang go unanswered, there's an assumption that the office is compromised and steps need to be taken to protect the data. He'll send men here. From what I understand, a lot of men."

"If that's true, why tell us? Why not wait for them to arrive, kill us, and free you?" Wayan asked in a manner that showed he didn't believe her.

"The unfortunate part of this protocol is that it dictates everyone dies. According to what Mr. Sanadi told me, this is because the general doesn't know what's going on or who he can trust. Therefore, the general's calls are answered immediately."

"They'd kill Sanadi for not answering his phone? I don't think so. That's a convenient lie," Tamala said. "They're not about to lose their money-laundering center."

"Hey, caveperson. I said that Sanadi and I were only sophisticated accountants backed up by an army of other professionals. We're the router. We're replaceable. I got Sanadi's job within the hour, didn't I? The general will send a bean counter or two from his staff in Beijing to temporarily replace me until he can find someone permanent. His Beijing staff knows the system. There won't be a burp in cash flow."

"Why isn't this operation in Beijing."

"You'll have to ask him, but I don't think he wants the Chinese government continually looking over his shoulder and risk exposing The Organization. Ensuring no one discovers the intricacies of what we're doing is, at least according to General Chao, more important than our lives."

"What do you suggest?" Wayan asked.

"Something that's going to be hard for you to swallow."

CHAPTER 11

FOLLOWING THREE FAILED attempts to get in touch with Woo and the four security guards assigned to the office, Chao phoned Kang and asked if he wanted to initiate their protocol.

"Wayan?" Kang asked, although it was more a statement than a question.

"Everything points to it. The last I heard from Woo, she was going to question him and Major Tamala and was sending her guards to kill Wayan's assistant."

"Strangely similar to what occurred at the warehouse." Chao agreed.

"I don't have to remind you that this upcoming transfer of money is critical for both of us."

"The required money is in the pipeline and will be wired on time. As I've repeatedly said, our cash-generating operations remain unchanged. I'll send an accounting team from my Beijing office to take over Sanadi and Woo's functions until we can find permanent replacements."

"Have you considered that destroying The Organization is Wayan's vendetta for attempting to kill him on the boat and at the warehouse? Besides taking down our clearinghouse, he might also be after the data in our computer system."

"We're the only ones who have unfiltered access to it. Even if he takes a computer or the server, he won't be able to hack it. He doesn't know anyone with that capability."

"Woo is a trove of information."

"I've written her off. Even temporarily, I need someone in that position who's strong, reliable, and gets things done - no matter what. That doesn't seem to be her. Since we don't offer a retirement plan - she, along with Wayan and anyone with him, will have to die."

"The sooner, the better. Initiate the protocol."

General Chien An was the Chief of the General Staff of the People's Liberation Army and a member of the Central Military Commission. He stood five feet, seven inches tall, had a stocky build with thick arms and legs, and an almost unnoticeable neck. He had the stature of a walking fire hydrant to many, although no one would say that to his face. He was currently looking at the electronic file on Woo that he received from army intelligence, which was generated because of the MSS intercept. After listening to the recording, he shook his head in disbelief.

Chao's predecessor, who had a Ph.D. in economics, had been high on diplomacy and short on performance. Subsequently, the Chinese government wired billions of dollars to support its neighbor. Chien An gave that general an early retirement and replaced him with Chao, who had a solid reputation for getting results.

Chao came to his attention not long after he was assigned as the commander of the Xinjiang Uyghur Autonomous Region in the northwest - a constant thorn in the side of Beijing. The area's residents had a history of verbally and physically attacking the government, both in the region and other cities. Although many in the government disagreed with Chao's methods of bringing the area under control, he got results. Insurgent activity in the northwest, and the export of terrorism to other cities, dropped to a trickle.

Seeing this, Chien An brought him to Beijing and gave him the additional duties of overseeing the Chinese side of North Korea's money-laundering operations - something his staff politely questioned because Chao had no financial experience. However, Chien An believed that success was about motivation, perseverance, and a refusal to fail rather than classroom learning. Since he was the highest military authority in the country, everyone fell in line when he reaffirmed his decision.

Chao proved to be a fast learner, and the cash flowing from Beijing to Pyongyang gradually stopped as the money laundering activities established by Chao, with Sanadi's help, rapidly expanded. Therefore, with his success in the northwest and North Korea's increased access to legal cash, Chien An wondered why he would torture and execute foreigners in Hong Kong. There was clearly a problem of which he wasn't aware. He wanted to call Chao and ask him directly, but he needed the unvarnished facts first. One name came to mind who could give that to him.

Chien An picked up his phone and called Lieutenant Colonel Yan He, his former aide and the one person he trusted without reservation. Stationed at the Raven Rock Mountain Complex in Pennsylvania, he was part of a joint US-China off-the-books team known as Nemesis. Following his latest mission, the lieutenant colonel was in Beijing on a two-week leave to see friends and rest before returning to his duty station.

Forty-five minutes after speaking to his former aide, Yan He entered the general's office. He was six feet, two inches tall, and had a swimmer's build with broad shoulders and a narrow waist. He had close-cropped black hair, black eyes, and virtually no sense of humor. The two exchanged pleasantries and had a cup of tea before Chien An let the lieutenant colonel hear the recording and gave him the electronic file on Woo.

"He could be trying to plug a problem in his money-laundering operation," Yan He offered, "and might be too embarrassed to tell you about it. Torturing those involved to see what they know and killing whoever was responsible for the problem fits that scenario. You and I would do the same."

"Perhaps. However, torturing and killing foreigners without my approval is unacceptable. That creates its own set of problems, not the least of which are friends and family knowing they came to Hong Kong in the passenger section of the aircraft and returned in the cargo hold. I don't want the state department of another country questioning our political leadership about what happened. This could have the unintended consequence of exposing Chao's money-laundering activities."

"The general has a reputation for being entrepreneurial in his problem-solving."

"I still need to know what's going on."

"With respect, you can ask him."

"I'd rather have the facts in front of me before that conversation."

"And you'd like me to get them for you?"

"I trust your tact and instincts."

"I'll need to make sure he's not in Hong Kong. If he is, I won't get anywhere."

"I'll handle that."

"When do I leave?"

Chien An didn't answer. Instead, he opened his desk drawer, removed an airline ticket, and handed it to him. "You won't have time to pack. Get whatever you need in Hong Kong."

The orders that Chao received from Chien An required him to return to Xinjiang immediately. This came as a surprise because he had an agreement with the general that his deputy would act in his stead while he oversaw his country's North Korean money laundering activities. Something changed that understanding, although he couldn't pinpoint what it might be. As Chien An's orders were unchallengeable, he had no choice but to follow them. However, he decided to push the envelope and delay his departure for two days. If Chien An found out, he'd think of a lie to tell him. He needed two days to straighten out the Hong Kong operation. He could have told him that Sanadi died in a car crash and that he sent an accounting team to Hong Kong to replace him temporarily. That would have been considered good management. Nevertheless, he was reluctant to involve Chien An because the general frequently asked the MSS to investigate deaths related to military activities, such as their money-laundering operation. The last thing he wanted was for them to request access to his server. Moreover, Chien An might decide to have them do a deep dive into the money laundering operation. If they did, they'd discover that he and his partners were siphoning billions performing an in-house function, yet claiming outside contractors cleaned the cash. Theft on this grand scale was not a crime that was survivable within the PRC. Therefore, he had to keep the situation under wraps - which required his presence in Beijing.

However, no sooner had Chao gone over the ramifications of discovery than he received two phone calls from Hong Kong. The source of the calls surprised him, but what they offered solved the problem of Wayan, his cohorts, and Melis Woo. If the caller were correct, he'd be able to disarm both minefields. After the second call, he phoned a PLA officer at the Hong Kong Garrison who performed discrete services for him in the past. He presented his problem, asked if he could solve it, and was told that he could - for a price. As Chao already had the man's offshore banking information, he wired the money.

A special administrative region, or SAR, is an autonomous region of China that has a separate legal, judicial, administrative, and economic system. It's also empowered to issue its own passports and adopt a language of its choosing. Hong Kong and Macau are SARs, and a passport is required for entry, even for Chinese citizens. However, in the Chinese Communist Party's thought process, autonomy doesn't mean independence. Therefore, a SAR still answers to Beijing, and its customs and immigration computers link to those on the mainland.

The "something that's going to be hard for you to swallow" statement made by Woo was accurate in that she offered, in exchange for her life, to get her four captors out of Hong Kong before General Chao's kill team arrived at the office. She estimated they had minutes to choose whether to trust her. Although no one was sure if Woo was lying to save her life, they agreed they couldn't take that chance and should leave quickly to avoid being caught on the 101st floor, where they had virtually no chance of escape. As Wayan pointed out, with Chao after them and Hong Kong's computers linked to mainland China, they couldn't leave Hong Kong without her help - if she was telling the truth.

Tamala upped the ante by telling her that if she were leading them into a trap, she would join Sanadi in the netherworld.

"Listen, cave dweller," Woo responded. "Chao wants to kill all of us. I have no loyalty to him."

Tamala shrugged. "Maybe. But my statement stands."

"What about the guards in our hotel room?" Eka asked Woo.

"Give me your room key."

Eka handed it over, and she tossed it on the conference room table. "Whoever arrives will solve that problem."

From the expressions on their faces, everyone understood what that meant.

"I'm not leaving without the server," Wayan said.

Not waiting for a response, he went to the data room, where he attempted to lift it from the rack. It didn't budge. Looking closely at the bottom of the server, he saw that a steel clamp held each side and that these were bolted to the rack. Because they were painted black, the same color as the server and rack, they were barely noticeable. Moreover, a black braided steel cable with a lock at the end ran through the metal-reinforced hole on the side of the server. If Wayan had a serious bolt cutter, he could cut the cable. However, to take the server, he would still need to unfasten a dozen screws in each of the steel clamps.

Wayan knew this type of security prevented a grab-and-run theft, where someone could slip the server under their jacket or in a backpack and walk out of the office with it at the end of the day. Now, the thief would need to walk down the office hall and past security guards with a pair of bolt cutters, then spend 15 minutes in the server room by themself - not the most discreet of thefts. Knowing that he didn't have the time required to take it, Wayan returned to the conference room, explained what he saw, and confronted Woo. "Why didn't you tell me?" he angrily asked.

"I've never been in the data room," Woo confessed. "But it sounds like something Sanadi would do." She looked at the time on her cell phone. "We're taking way too long. We need to get out of here immediately."

Leading the way to the front door, Woo stopped by her office and grabbed her purse, hidden in a compartment inside her desk. Not trusting there wasn't a weapon inside, Tamala grabbed and searched it, finding a cell phone charging cable, wallet, lipstick, and other personal items within. He handed the purse back, after which Woo grabbed her Burberry raincoat and hat from behind the door and left her office.

They took the elevator to the lobby and then got into a taxi, where Woo told the driver to take them to the LYC, which every taxi driver knew was short for the Lantau Yacht Club. It was evident that she was a member when the guard at the entry gate raised the barrier upon seeing her and allowed the taxi to proceed to the clubhouse. The square two-story structure, painted entirely in white, had large view windows facing the marina, which had 148 slips and 38 superyacht berths.

Entering the clubhouse, the receptionists recognized Woo, one getting up from their chair and escorting the group into a large lounge.

"Everyone here seems to know you," Wayan said. "Do you own a boat?"

"No, but looking at them and the water beyond is calming. Trust me, Wayan, laundering money is stressful. I come here every day after leaving the office to have dinner and wind down."

"I probably would as well."

"I need to make a few phone calls and use the computer in one of the business rooms to complete our departure arrangements," Woo said. "Clean up and get something to eat and drink while we wait."

"Wait for what?" Wayan asked.

"Transport." Without further explanation, she proceeded to the restroom.

On her return, she walked past them and into the first of three business rooms at the edge of the lounge. Each was ten feet long and six feet wide. Inside was a small desk, on top of which was a computer and inkjet printer. Because there was a glass door, anyone in the lounge could see inside.

Wayan and the rest of his team followed and sat at the table closest to Woo's room, approximately 20 feet away.

"She's up to something," Wayan said.

"You mean, besides getting us out of Hong Kong alive," Eka responded.

"Yes."

"Why do you say that?"

"Because she's not scared. I would be. And why is she carrying that raincoat and hat? It's hot, and we're running for our lives, at least according to her. That makes little sense."

"It's a double-breasted paneled Burberry trench coat," Eka said. "It sells for over $4,000. No woman is going to leave that behind."

"Why would anyone need to buy a coat that expensive?"

"Because they want to look nice. My slacks and blouse are Burberry. Do you think I paid too much for these?"

Tamala and Nabar, decorated special forces officers, were not brave enough to get dragged into the middle of that discussion. Looking away, they were content to let Wayan dig his own grave. Thankfully, a server came to the table and asked for their membership card. Seeing what was happening, Woo stepped out of the room and pointed to herself, indicating the service should be billed to her account. The server got the message and began handing out menus and taking orders.

The alcohol arrived first, with the men receiving their Bintang beers and Eka an Aperol Spritz. Twenty minutes later, their food arrived, and the server deftly brought another round of drinks with it. Wayan had earlier asked Woo what she wanted, only to be told she wasn't hungry.

Woo continued to use the computer for the next 40 minutes, after which she grabbed her coat and hat and went to where everyone was seated. Her timing was good as the server just finished clearing the table. She dragged a chair from an adjoining table and squeezed it in between Wayan and Tamala, who both moved their chairs to give her space.

"Our transport will be here in less than an hour," Woo said, looking at the large circular clock across the room.

"Where are we going?" Wayan asked.

"Macau. A casino hotel owner owes me some rather large favors, and I'm going to collect."

"Favors such as helping him launder money?" Wayan asked.

"You're wasting brainpower in your current occupation, Wayan. I could show you how to make serious money if you joined me on the dark side, as they say."

"I'd be a criminal."

"But a very rich one." Seeing from the lack of enthusiasm on his face that it would never happen, she continued with the business at hand. "No matter. This is how it's going to work. The casino will send its yacht to pick us up. Once we arrive in Hong Kong, a driver will escort you to a limo."

"Don't we need to clear customs and immigration in both places?" Nabar asked.

"Normally, we'd stop by the customs and immigration office at Shun Tak Centre in Sheung Wan, and at the Taipa Ferry Terminal in Macau, to get the required stamps. However, since we're trying to stay below General Chao's radar, you'll be taken ashore at a local dock where a limo will bring us to the hotel."

"How do we leave Macau without our passports being stamped?" Wayan asked.

"Two aircraft will arrive within 48 hours. One will take you and your friends to Indonesia, where you'll use your passports to enter the country. The casino we're going to will place a Hong Kong exit stamp, along with Macau entry and exit stamps, on them so that Indonesian immigration won't freak out."

"And the second aircraft?" Wayan asked.

"That's mine. It will take me to the first of several destinations. I'll be switching identities and modes of transport along the way until I eventually arrive at my bolt hole."

"This is well thought out," Eka conceded. "It's not a spur-of-the-moment plan."

"I put together several escape plans when I accepted the job of Sanadi's assistant, knowing that I might need to leave at a moment's notice. When you deal with people as ruthless as Kang and Chao, a stealthy and quick departure is the only way to leave The Organization and remain alive."

"If most of this was preplanned, why were you in that room for so long?" Wayan asked. "Contacting a casino operator and an aircraft charter service doesn't take 40 minutes, nor probably the use of your computer. As you said, you put together several escape plans. You wouldn't rely on having a computer connection for your escape. You'd make a few phone calls."

"Figure it out."

Wayan thought about for a few seconds. "Whatever you were up to was about you and something you had to do before you went to your bolt hole, as you called it."

"Go on."

"It's a warm day, yet you were insistent on taking your raincoat and hat when you left your office. Even a Burberry coat and hat wouldn't be monetarily significant since I assume you've made a pile of cash from laundering money within and outside The Organization. You could easily buy replacements. It's not the coat and hat that are important but what's hidden in them."

"Brilliant. Continue."

"I looked in the pockets and patted the coat and hat down. There was nothing in either," Tamala interrupted.

"Have you figured this conundrum out?" Woo asked Wayan with a smile.

"I think so. The raincoat and hat contained information essential for you to access your money. I assume, if Major Tamala couldn't feel it, that it's written on paper or fabric and hidden in the clothing."

"Fabric," Woo confirmed. "It doesn't make a crunching sound when someone squeezes it. It's not just my accounts that are on the fabric, Wayan."

"It's the names and addresses of banks, financial institutions, and other entities holding the laundered money for The Organization, along with the passwords, account names, and numbers," Wayan answered, walking down the road Woo laid for him."

"Close. Refine what you just said. Think about how you'd do this and take a slightly more cautious approach."

Wayan altered what he'd previously said. "From what you told us about the enormous number of banks, account numbers, passwords, attorneys, and middlemen, you'd need a bolt of fabric to copy down all that information, not to mention the time it would take to keep it current. My guess is that you're electronically storing this information on a site to which you memorized the internet address and password. What you're carrying is the most critical component - the passwords. You didn't want to have everything in one location. The passwords aren't on the site."

"A solid analysis, and correct. I could make you a billionaire. You're working for pennies."

"This was always your end game," Wayan said, ignoring Woo's offer.

"Always. You pushed ahead my timeline before I could put the last piece of my plan in place. I'll do that in short order."

"Tell me what happens when The Organization finds out that you've looted their bank accounts, which I'm assuming you plan to do?"

"Those accounts, the accounts of their founders, North Korea, and Kim Jong-un and his family."

"Kim Jong-un?" Wayan asked in astonishment.

"The Organization diverted billions to his accounts and that of his family. Remember, all laundered cash flowed through our clearinghouse, and I'm the one who established these accounts and wired money to them. Therefore, I know how to access every account and, even if they change their passwords, I have a backdoor into each with a master passcode."

"It's easy to send money into an account, but getting it out is another matter."

"I'm the one who set up these accounts. I frequently wire money in and out."

"How much money are you going to take?"

"Twenty-three-billion and change. And it's already done." Woo smiled, seeing the shock on everyone's face.

"They'll come looking for you with a vengeance," Nabar said.

"With every sleuth, assassin, and low life that they can employ. But it will be to no avail. My bolt hole will be secure and undiscoverable. Besides, the search won't last long. Kang will have to explain to Kim Jong-un where his money went. He'll never believe he wasn't involved in the theft. You don't have to ask how that conversation will end."

"And Chao?'

"I have something special in mind for him."

"Sanadi wasn't the brains of this operation; you were," Eka said.

"Look who just woke up. Brava. I happily gave him credit for everything I created because, with him in the spotlight, I bypassed the scrutiny he was always under."

A tone on Woo's phone interrupted their conversation. She took the call and told the person they would be right there.

"The yacht is docking," Woo said. She then led the way through the clubhouse and onto the guest dock.

CHAPTER 12

LIEUTENANT COLONEL YAN He arrived at the Hong Kong airport and took a taxi to the business entrance of the International Commerce Center. He'd left his uniform in Beijing and changed into civilian clothes because Chinese military uniforms seemed to cause consternation with Hong Kong residents. His choice of attire was a dark blue blazer, khaki pants, and a white shirt.

Upon arriving at the ICC, he went to the security desk where, after showing his PLA officer ID card to the rent-a-cop, he was issued a pass and proceeded through the turnstile. Taking the elevator to the 101st floor, he went to suite 10104 and pressed the buzzer outside the office. Eventually, a gruff male voice came through the intercom box and asked what he wanted. Yan He identified himself and, in an authoritative voice, said that he needed to enter.

"This office only answers to General Hulin Chao," the gruff voice replied with a note of arrogance.

"I'm here at the direction of General Chien An, chief of the general staff of the People's Liberation Army. There is no higher military authority. I can conference him, you, and General Chao so that we can get past this impasse. However, I can't guarantee where your next assignment might be."

131

The lock was released, and Yan He opened the door.

There were six people inside the office. One was in Sanadi's room, one in Woo's, and four in the conference room, two of whom wore cheap business suits too tight for their muscular frames. Yan He assumed they were the muscle. The gruff voice was standing to the right of the muscle. He was thin, five feet, seven inches tall, and looked to be in his mid-50s.

"Why are you here, colonel?" the gruff voice demanded.

"That's my question to you."

"General Chao sent us to audit this facility. It's routine."

"So routine that the audit is being conducted without the office staff present? Shouldn't they be here to assist?"

"Those questions are best answered by General Chao."

"How long have you and your colleagues been here?"

"Not long."

"And where did you come from?"

"Beijing."

"Not Hong Kong?"

"We're part of General Chao's...." The man hesitated, trying to find a description for his job while not mentioning money laundering.

"The North Korean Monetary Assistance Program," Yan He said, finishing the man's sentence - instantly relieving the anxiety of the person in front of him.

"You're not here to audit the facility; you're here to manage it."

The man didn't respond, letting Yan He's statement stand.

"Who's usually in charge of this office."

"Kulon Sanadi. He recently died in an auto accident."

"And his assistant, Melis Woo?"

"Gone."

"The guards assigned to this office?"

"Dead."

"How?"

"I'd rather not say."

"Are any of you auditors?"

"Two. They're in the offices."

"And the others?"

"He and I are administrative support staff," the man said, pointing to the person beside him. "They're security," he concluded by nodding towards the muscular men.

"Is this a temporary or permanent assignment for the six of you?"

"Unknown," the man conceded.

"Go back to what you were doing. I'm going to look around," Yan He said as he brushed by the man and began talking with the muscle.

Forty-five minutes later, he finished speaking with everyone, confirming they were here because the prior office staff was dead or gone. He was about to inspect the rooms when the gruff voice approached him. He appeared to be relaxed, a sharp contrast to his previous demeanor.

"General Chao sends his regards. He's directed everyone to give you our undivided support."

Yan He thanked him, although what he said sounded perfunctory rather than heartfelt. Yan He didn't believe it. Something was going on.

A search of the conference room cabinets, offices, kitchen, and bathroom went quickly and yielded nothing. Entering the data room, he saw the black boxes. However, after examining each, he found that neither had a USB port. That meant he couldn't transfer what was on them to the hard drive he had in his jacket pocket, which the general gave him. Therefore, he had to take the black boxes with him. However, after seeing how they were attached to the rack, he knew that would not be easy.

Returning to the conference room, he told the man with a gruff voice that he was taking the data room equipment.

"You can't do that."

"You said General Chao told you to give me your undivided support."

"But not to remove equipment."

"Are you telling me you don't have a backup of this data and can't tap into it?"

The man didn't answer, knowing that the lieutenant colonel's next step would be to call General Chien An, which would conflict with his instructions from Chao.

"Take the equipment," the gruff voice responded.

"One last thing. I'll need tools to remove it from the rack. Are there any in the office?"

The gruff voice went to the rear of the conference room, took the toolbox off the floor, and handed it to him without comment.

When Yan He returned to the data room, he opened the toolbox and rummaged through it. "These wire cutters couldn't cut chicken wire," he commented to himself, throwing them back in the box after inspecting its blades. "But this might work." He pulled out a pair of needle-nose pliers.

Yan He disconnected the power to the black boxes and gently worked the tip of the pliers beneath the plastic server case, next to the metal-reinforced hole through which the cable ran. Breaking away a tiny piece of the case at a time, he eventually took away the plastic around the reinforced hole until it separated from the server case. He repeated the process for the box below, afterward removing the screws from the four steel clamps securing the equipment.

Going into the kitchen, he returned with a cardboard box that he'd seen earlier and placed the two black boxes within it. The gruff voice was standing outside the door when he left the data room.

"I'll try to get these back to you as quickly as possible after our techs in Beijing examine them," Yan He said.

"As you pointed out, we have a backup of this data. We'll make do."

That response was far too cooperative, leading him to suspect that General Chao was up to something. He was right.

Yan He initially planned on spending the night in Hong Kong, having no idea how long his inspection of the money-laundering office would take. However, as the search took a fraction of the time expected, he wanted to return to Beijing with the two black boxes as quickly as possible, hoping they would clarify the recording that Chien An received. There was no doubt the general had someone who could extract their contents. Unit 61398, one of the most sophisticated hacking groups in the world, was under his command. They often broke into the complicated computer systems of nation-states and multinational corporations, retrieving data that some would have said was impossible to get. Since there were no paper files, these electronic devices were the only items of informational value in suite 10104. His mission was complete.

Looking at an app on his cell phone, he saw one remaining flight from Hong Kong to Beijing, which departed in two hours and twenty minutes. Since he was only 30 minutes from the airport, he'd use the extra time to make a stop at one of the airport's sundry shops to buy a carry-on bag, not wanting to carry a box which was falling apart onto the aircraft.

When he arrived at the gate, with the carry-on bag he'd purchased, he saw that there were relatively few passengers waiting to board. This was in line with the ticket agent telling him that the aircraft was 20 percent occupied. Therefore, passengers could sit wherever they wanted since this configuration had no first or business class sections.

Boarding began 40 minutes before their scheduled departure time, which was standard for the airline but made no sense to Yan He given the number of passengers. After putting his canvas bag in the overhead bin, he selected 38F, a window seat near the rear of the aircraft. He hoped most would prefer to sit in the front, which would allow them to get off the plane quickly and clear customs and immigration faster. Sitting in the rear offered the possibility that he would get some sleep.

He expected that tomorrow would be a long day and he needed all the sleep he could get. Chien An was an early riser and always entered his office promptly at 6:00 a.m. Therefore, he needed to be at the August 1st building 15 minutes before then.

The plane took off 22 minutes early and, immediately after a quick beverage service, the flight attendants dimmed the overhead lights. Yan He reclined his seat, covered himself with a thin airline blanket, and fell asleep before the aircraft leveled off at 37,000 feet.

Somewhere over Wuhan, a passenger switched from seat 43A to 39F - the seat directly behind the lieutenant colonel who, by this time, was fast asleep. Yan He's head was canted to the right, resting against the window. To get into this comfortable position, he removed his seatbelt.

The man who was now seated in seat 39F looked around and verified that he and the person in front of him were the only passengers at the rear of the aircraft. He removed from his pocket a light gray plastic case with a black safety cap, identical to a Sharpie, which was the designer's intent. Looking through the gap between the seat and the right bulkhead, against which Yan He rested his head, the man saw the nape of the lieutenant colonel's neck. Taking the marker-like instrument, he removed the protective cap, careful not to touch the felt tip. Extending it through the gap in front of him, he lightly ran it across both sides of the lieutenant colonel's neck. When he was through, he carefully recapped the instrument, put it back in his jacket pocket, and returned to seat 43A.

The plane landed in Beijing 37 minutes ahead of schedule, and the passengers disembarked quickly. The man in 43A was the last to leave, and as he passed row 38, he grabbed the canvas bag that he watched Yan He place into the overhead bin. He then continued to the forward hatch and left the aircraft.

The man's stride was long, and his pace fast as he strode into the immigration queue. Once his passport was stamped, he continued his lengthy stride and fast pace through baggage claim, slowing only to clear the customs officer, and continued out of the airport terminal.

As the fast-paced man was passing through customs, one of the flight attendants on board the flight from Hong Kong was checking that no one was in the restrooms or was asleep in their seat. Both were common occurrences on international flights. As the flight attendant was on their way to check the rear restrooms, it never occurred to her to look down. Therefore, she didn't see the six feet, two inches tall man lying on the deck of the aircraft - the result of unfastening his seat belt and the generous braking employed by the pilot to get off at the first taxiway and shorten the time to the gate. However, on the flight attendant's return trip down the aisle, she was looking for carry-on baggage placed under the seat and forgotten. Looking down row 38, she saw Yan He's expressionless face staring at her.

Following the flight attendant's scream, the other crew members came running.

"Call the paramedics," the captain said to the copilot as he knelt beside Yan He and held a finger to his wrist, checking for a pulse. Finding none, he pulled him into the aisle and began CPR.

Two minutes later, a paramedic team boarded the aircraft, and the captain stopped his efforts. The paramedics, failing to detect a heartbeat, ripped his shirt open, powered up the defibrillation paddles, and tried to shock his heart back to life. However, getting no response to their third electroshock, they pronounced Yan He dead. The body was carried off the aircraft to a waiting gurney and transported to the morgue. The paramedics wrote in their report that they believed the cause of death to be a myocardial infarction, the medical term for a heart attack, with no evidence of foul play.

CHAPTER 13

GENERAL CHIEN AN arrived at his office at 6:00 a.m. His routine from that point never varied. It started with a cup of green tea brought to his desk by his senior aide, the lieutenant colonel who replaced Yan He. The aide, who had been at the office for two hours by the time his boss arrived, handed the general a thick folder containing printouts of emails and other communique placed in the order of their military classifications, with the highest priority on top. The general preferred looking at a piece of paper rather than a computer screen. The aide would leave the office once the tea and folders were delivered. Today, however, he broke that routine and, instead of leaving, he cleared his throat. This caused Chien An, sitting in his desk chair, to look up and notice the nervous expression on his face.

"Is there something else?"

"Sir, if you'll look at the top page in the folder, you'll see that airport security notified the army of the death of Lieutenant Colonel Yan He."

Those words stunned the general as much as if he was hit with a bucket of cold water. He pulled the page from the folder and read it. Once he finished, his face displayed an intense rage.

"The lieutenant colonel is scheduled for an autopsy today. We'll know more when the doctor gives us his report," the aide continued.

"Stop the autopsy and have the body transported from wherever it is to Hospital 301. You will accompany Lieutenant Colonel Yan He and never leave him unattended until he arrives at that hospital. Is that understood?"

The aide replied it was.

"Arrange for an honor guard to accompany you. Other than for transport, no one is to touch the lieutenant colonel's body. No one. I'll handle the arrangements at the hospital," the general said in a stern voice. "If anyone disputes these orders, have them call me. Before they do, tell them to dress warm, they're going to need it where I'm sending them."

The aide, who never saw the general display such anger, acknowledged his orders and sprinted from the office.

Once he left, Chien An slammed his fist down on the desk. The force of the blow causing some of the tea to spill from his cup.

Yan He had been his aide for three years. During that time, he developed a fondness for the no-nonsense 37-year-old lieutenant colonel, who he would later appoint to Nemesis. He was an exemplary officer in every respect. He didn't believe for a second that his death was from a heart attack. He died because he was transporting two black boxes from Chao's Hong Kong clearinghouse - and nothing was going to convince him otherwise. He was going to find out who was involved with his death and kill everyone who thought they could get away with murdering such an honorable man who served his country.

Focusing on the present, he realized he needed to arrange for the autopsy at Hospital 301 before his aide arrived with the body. Looking at the contact list on his phone, he found the number for the administrator. The hospital, which catered to high-ranking members of the Chinese Communist Party, had the finest medical staff and most modern equipment of any medical facility in China.

The administrator answered Chien An's call after half a dozen rings, sounding as if he'd just woken up because he had. When the general identified himself, a shot of adrenalin went through his system, and he sat upright in bed.

The administrator listened as Chien An said that his aide would arrive with the body of Lieutenant Colonel Yan He, and he wanted an autopsy performed by the most competent forensic doctor on his staff. Once the intrusion into his former aide's body was complete, he told him how the remains were to be handled. The administrator was writing what he'd been told on a notepad that he kept on the nightstand beside his bed, his handwriting no better than most of the doctors working at the hospital.

During their call, the general didn't ask for his advice and he wasn't about to give any since he and the hospital staff were part of the PLA, and Chien An was at the top of that food chain. As Hospital 301 was the Beverly Hills of Chinese medical facilities, and a black mark on his record by the general would end his career, the administrator was hellbent to ensure that everything went smoothly. He called the hospital duty officer and ordered that a gurney and medical team wait outside the ambulance entrance for Yan He's remains to arrive. The administrator then phoned a staff forensic pathologist, who had a reputation for being a stickler for details and a genius at determining unapparent causes of death, and told him he was going to perform an autopsy this morning. Although this was his day off and he was asleep when the administrator called, he was ordered to get to the hospital as quickly as possible. The physician, two ranks below the administrator, didn't argue and arrived ten minutes before Chien An's aide, Yan He's body, and the honor guard accompanying it.

Chien An believed that his former aide's death, just after he went to the clearinghouse, was no coincidence and that he was murdered. Therefore, he discovered something, or was close to it, and needed to be silenced. There weren't many people who had the nerve or the power to order a lieutenant colonel in the PLA to be killed. General Hulin Chao was at the top of that list. But he needed proof, which he believed was in the devices that Yan He carried with him. He summoned one of his four administrative staff.

"Call China Airlines and ask if anything was left on board the flight that Yan He took to Beijing. He was carrying something, and I want to know if they have it."

The staff member left the office and, ten minutes later, returned and said that the airline reported nothing was left on board by any of the passengers. The general didn't like what he heard. If his former aide was returning with two black boxes, where were they? He reasoned that could only mean that someone on his flight took it - the same person who killed him.

Although there were no security cameras within the aircraft, the Hong Kong and Beijing airports had an extensive system. He again summoned an aide, with another staff member responding.

"Get me the passenger and crew manifests for the Air China flight that Lieutenant Colonel Yan He took last night and run those names through our national database to see what we have on each person. Next, get the video feeds from the Hong Kong airport showing the lieutenant colonel from the moment he arrived until he boarded the aircraft. I also want to see the feeds from the Capital International Airport showing passengers and crew from the time they disembarked the flight, passed through customs and immigration, and left the terminal."

Knowing that the general was in a hurry, the aide divided these tasks with the rest of the staff. It took the four staff members 30 minutes to retrieve what Chien An requested. Air China, and the security offices at the Hong Kong and Beijing airports, provided what was asked for without hesitation because the military requested it. The staff printed this information, except for the airport security footage, for which they provided the relevant links.

Chien An read that there were 38 passengers and five crew, which excluded the lieutenant colonel. He eliminated the pilot, copilot, and the three flight attendants because they were scheduled for this flight weeks in advance, and none could have known that the lieutenant colonel would be on it. Going through the passenger manifest and looking at their backgrounds, he broke them into categories. Twenty were married and traveling with their spouse. Twelve were over 65 years of age and traveling by themselves. Three were children, and two were monks. The last person, Captain Shum Win, assigned to the PLA's Hong Kong Garrison, didn't fit into any of these categories. On a hunch, he asked one of the staff to find if the captain had booked a future flight from Beijing to Hong Kong, assuming that he'd have a return flight since he was stationed at the garrison. Three minutes later, he received an answer.

"He's on this morning's 9:30 a.m. flight to Hong Kong."

"Considering he'd have to clear customs and immigration coming into and leaving the mainland, that means he was only here for a few hours. Why?"

"Do you want him brought here?" the staff member asked.

Chien An thought for a few seconds. "No. I know where to find him. Have my car brought around; I'm going to Hospital 301."

General Hulin Chao met with Captain Shum Win at his office in the Ministry of National Defense building, roughly eight miles and change from Chien An's office. The purpose of the meeting was to hand over whatever Yan He carried on board. Shum Win never looked inside the carry-on he retrieved, even though he was tempted, because he didn't want to know what was in it. Given that he killed a lieutenant colonel to get what was in the bag, looking inside might make him the next casualty.

"Are you sure this was what he was carrying? An athletic bag?" Chao asked, looking at the canvas carry-on with HVAA embroidered on the side. HVAA an abbreviation for the Happy Valley Athletic Association, a famous soccer club.

"I saw him carrying this onto the aircraft, and only one person was standing between us when he placed it into the overhead bin. Other than when I killed the lieutenant colonel, I had my eyes on that bin the entire time. This is his bag."

Chao opened it. Reaching into the carry-on, he was expressionless as he removed a 1/24 diecast scale model of a Chinese SX2150 general utility truck. "This doesn't look like a server," Chao said, the tone of his voice reflecting disappointment and anger.

"That's what he carried on the plane. I swear!" Shum Win said, the pitch of his voice elevating slightly.

Chao went to his couch, sat down, and said nothing for five minutes. When he spoke, his voice was devoid of emotion, which was unusual for the impulsive general known for his hair-trigger temper. Judging from the fear on Shum Win's face, he found this lack of emotion to be more frightening than his outbursts.

"Yan He was clever. Before the plane took off, he sent the server to the only person he trusted - General Chien An."

Shum Win remained silent as beads of sweat formed on his forehead.

"I have another task for you. Tomorrow, at 2:00 p.m., at the Macau private air terminal, a Gulfstream G450 will arrive to transport Melis Woo to an unknown destination. As difficult as it is for me not to put a bullet in her head, I want you to kill her in the same manner that you dispatched the lieutenant colonel. Don't cause a scene. There will be too many questions about who she is and what she did if she dies violently. Your military ID will get you into the terminal. Here is her picture," Chao said, handing the two-by-two-inch photo to him. "That bitch screwed me," Chao volunteered. "She phoned me twice; we made a deal for her to turn over Wayan, his assistant, and the two others helping him. In return, I wired her $10 million, after which she goes silent and won't return my calls."

Shum Win put the photo in his pocket. "Do you want me to kill Wayan and those with him?"

"I'll have Basri's replacement do it once they're back in Indonesia. They'll be easy to find. Again, killing them in Hong Kong or Macau will generate too many questions. In Indonesia, no one will care."

When Shum Win left the office, Chao went to his laptop computer and looked at the email sent to his non-military account. It provided the date, time, and mode of transport that Melis Woo would use to leave Macau. The name at the bottom was that of Gunter Wayan. He asked that he and his associates be left alone in exchange for providing this information and developing amnesia as to everything they saw or heard.

"And, at the right time, I'll make sure that amnesia becomes permanent," Chao said to himself as he closed the lid of his laptop.

Chien An waited in the VIP lounge surrounded by the hospital's administrator and a dozen general officers who worked with Yan He and came to honor him. They drank gallons of coffee, smoked packs of cigarettes, even though non-smoking signs were posted throughout the room, and told stories that brought back fond memories of the lieutenant colonel. Eventually, they left and returned to their commands leaving only Chien An and the administrator until the doctor who performed the autopsy entered the lounge.

"One of the stranger autopsies I've conducted," he began. "A constriction of both carotid arteries, which cut the blood flow to his brain, caused his death. I've ordered a toxicology screen."

"Was he killed?" Chien An asked.

"It's unusual for both arteries to close rapidly and simultaneously without an outside influence."

"Could he have ingested a poison?"

"I don't believe the toxicology screen will show that he ingested or inhaled a poison or toxin. The vasoconstriction was localized to his carotids and didn't affect either his respiratory or digestive systems."

"Vasoconstriction?"

"A narrowing of the blood vessels resulting from the contraction of the muscular wall of the vessels. In this situation, the carotid arteries constricted to closure."

"What outside influences, as you called them, can cause both arteries to close simultaneously?"

"A vasoconstrictive topical compound that's absorbed through the skin."

"You're saying, in medical terminology, that someone put this topical on each of the lieutenant colonel's carotids, with a glove or something that would avoid it coming in contact with their skin."

"That's my preliminary belief."

"Wouldn't he feel it?"

"Not necessarily. It wouldn't take much of the topical since it only went over two vessels."

"Have you seen this type of vasoconstrictive occurrence before?"

"I have. I autopsied someone last year who put it on their face believing it was medication."

"A horrible death."

"A horrible death," the doctor agreed.

"I'll find the manufacturer and ask for a list of their distributors. Once I have that information, I'll find the buyer."

"It won't be difficult to find the manufacturer. And there's no distributor because this vasoconstrictive is not for sale."

"It isn't?"

"No. The PLA manufactures it, and the person who put it on their face worked in a chemical warfare laboratory."

Chien An entered his office and saw a China Airlines box sitting on his desk.

"What's this?" he asked one of his assistants.

"The airline delivered it while you were out. The sender's name isn't on the box, but it passed through the building's explosive, biological, and radiological scanners. Would you like me to open it?"

"No, I'll do it. Close the door behind you."

Once his aide left, he removed a folding knife from the top drawer of his desk and cut through the plastic sealing tape. Inside, he found the two black boxes that Yan He had taken.

"Even death didn't stop you from completing your assignment. I'm going to miss you."

After giving himself a moment to pull it together, Chien An called the head of Unit 61398, the army's elite hacking unit. He told the major who answered that he needed the information inside a server and assumed it had a high level of encryption.

"I'll send someone to get it."

"Can you hack it?"

"We rarely encounter data that doesn't have encryption using algorithms that portend to be unbreakable. If we're not talking the NSA or nation-state encryption, with our sophisticated hacking tools and supercomputers, we should be able to give you the unencrypted data."

"How long will it take?"

"You'll have it by the end of the day."

That estimate was correct.

CHAPTER 14

T WAS 1:30 p.m. the day following his meeting with Chao when Shum Win, dressed in a tan business suit with an open-collared white shirt, both of which he purchased the previous day, entered the private air terminal at the Macau airport. He approached the attractive lady at the reception desk and said that he was awaiting a business associate and asked if he could sit in the lounge until his aircraft landed. The woman gave him a warm smile and said he could stay as long as he wanted. Getting up from her chair, she escorted him into the plush lounge. Once he was seated, she offered him a beverage of his choice, which he declined. She then returned to her desk.

The lounge's floor-to-ceiling glass windows looked onto the tarmac of the private terminal. Parked approximately 30 yards away from the building were two aircraft - a Gulfstream G450 and a Cessna 750 Citation X. On the far side of the lounge, near the restrooms and a door marked *Staff Only,* five people sat around a circular table. In front of them were empty coffee cups and the remains of snacks from the food and beverage bar. Carry-on bags, some with wheels and some without, were bunched against a wall near the table.

Shum Win started towards Woo, although it looked as if he was going to the restroom. As he walked, he removed the Sharpie-like instrument from his pocket and pulled off its plastic safety cap. He didn't concern himself with the four people surrounding her. His orders were to ignore them and be nonconfrontational in bringing about her death. Therefore, he planned to trip as he neared her table and fall into her, two swipes, one over each carotid artery, an apology, and he was out the door and into his car. Six miles later, he would cross the border into Zhuhai, China. After that, it was a 30-mile drive to the airport where Chao had a plane waiting.

Woo was engrossed in conversation with those around her and didn't seem to notice his approach. She was wearing a blouse that was cut low enough to expose the upper part of her neck. Perfect times two.

Shum Win gripped the instrument tightly in his right hand as he approached Woo's chair. Another twelve inches, and he'd accidentally trip into his victim. As he extended his right foot to begin his fall, she disappeared, replaced by a yellow light that quickly transformed to white. As this was happening, he heard a humming sound and felt himself falling to the floor in slow motion. That was the last sensation he would ever experience.

Wayan, Eka, Tamala, and Nabar were sitting with Woo. Everyone was waiting for the pilots to finish filing their flight plans and complete their pre-flight checks before heading to their aircraft. As they waited, a well-dressed man walked towards them. This wasn't unusual because everyone going to the restroom walked near their table. Therefore, they ignored him - almost. What caught their attention was that he opened his jacket and took out a Sharpie, at least that's what it looked like from a distance, and removed the cap. Woo, unconcerned, adjusted the napkin on her lap and continued her conversation with Nabar, who was to her left. Ten feet from the table, the man altered his path and headed towards them. Behind him, the receptionist was showing someone the lounge, and they were also coming towards their table. From the serious looks on their faces, neither were relaxed.

When the man got to within two feet of Woo, she turned and locked eyes with the stranger, sliding her right hand under her napkin as she did. However, she quickly shifted her focus to the receptionist and the older gentleman with her. Both had handguns with silencers aimed at her, or so she thought until they put two rounds into the back of Shum Win's head. The PLA captain, his right arm extended with the Sharpie-like instrument in his hand, collapsed onto the carpet beside Woo's chair.

Because the powerful rounds exited the man's head, blood and brain matter splattered over a wide section of carpet and the back of two chairs. However, it missed the five people at the table, who remained frozen as the older man approached the body and, with a look of hate and disgust, put six Parabellum rounds into the corpse's torso.

"It seems that Captain Shum Win committed suicide," Chien An said to the attractive woman beside him, who was a PLA intelligence agent posing as the receptionist. "I'm sure he had an encounter with a prostitute from one of the casinos and was desolate when he learned she was seeing someone else."

"That's the way the autopsy and field report will read. I'll have the body removed," the woman said.

The facial expressions on the five people sitting around the table seemed to say they doubted a coroner would view two rounds in the back of his head and six body shots as a suicide. However, since they weren't the ones holding the guns, they were ready to swear to the authorities that it was indeed a suicide.

Chien An placed his silenced Type 77 handgun in his shoulder holster and bent down and picked up the applicator for the vasoconstrictor.

"So that's how they did it," he said, carefully placing the plastic cap over the tip before putting the Sharpie in his jacket pocket. "I'm sure you'd like an explanation," the general said as he brought a chair from an adjoining table and placed it next to Woo. Everyone moved to give him space. He introduced himself, and everyone at the table did the same.

Chien An started by saying that he sent his former aide to the Hong Kong office after receiving the recording of a conversation between Chao and Woo. That prompted him to investigate what was going on.

Woo, shaking her head, conceded she must have used her phone instead of Sanadi's to make that call. "I wasn't thinking," she admitted. "Sanadi told me that his phone had an unbreakable encryption and to use it if I ever spoke with General Chao."

Chien An continued by telling them how Yan He got the server to him and that a unit under his command hacked it.

"It revealed that Chao, Kang, and Sanadi, along with a host of others, were profiting from the clearinghouse operations. After that," Chien An said, "I asked them to hack General Chao's computers, personal and military, and retrieve his emails. That's how I learned that all of you would be in Macau and that the general would send someone to kill Ms. Woo."

"Then we were in your protective cocoon the entire time," Eka said.

"I wouldn't say that, but given what I knew was about to happen, I arranged for the private air terminal's staff to take the day off and canceled incoming and outgoing charter flights to Macau."

"Why didn't you arrest the killer, assassin, or whatever you want to call him when he entered the building? Why let him get close to Woo?" Wayan asked.

"The man's name was Captain Shum Win. I wanted to see how he planned to kill Ms. Woo and needed to be sure that this was the same person who murdered Lieutenant Colonel Yan He. If he wasn't, that meant I still needed to find them. And, for your information, I was never going to arrest him."

"You're an excellent shot for an old man," Woo said, bringing a smile to everyone's face.

"One thing I don't understand," Eka stated. "From what Ms. Woo told us, I thought an RSA digital key was required to access the clearinghouse server and that it was unhackable without it. Did General Chao's computer also require a digital key? How did get around that?"

Chien An explained that only the clearinghouse computers and server used an RSA key. Chao's government and personal computers had an encryption chip embedded into them, and that both could receive unencrypted emails. He went on to say that since the encryption chips were designed by the government and issued to the PLA, his hacking unit had the decryption software to look at every email Chao sent and received.

"That tells us how you accessed his computers but not how you got into the clearinghouse server," Tamala said.

"As it was explained to me, Chao had a 768-bit RSA system, which was what the PLA used when he set up the clearinghouse. While it was state of the art at the time, it's now old technology. Therefore, my hacking unit's supercomputers had no difficulty cracking it. The newer larger bit systems, which the government uses and hasn't yet issued to the military, is theoretically uncrackable - for now."

"Let's go back. You said you learned General Chao was sending someone to kill Woo in Macau by hacking his computer. There are only five people who knew she'd be at the private air terminal on this day and at this time. Myself and the four sitting next to me. Can you explain how Chao found out?" Wayan asked.

"It was the email from you, Mr. Wayan. It asked, in exchange for this information, that everyone except for Ms. Woo be allowed to leave Macau and return to Indonesia unharmed."

"I never sent that email."

"I know you didn't."

"I sent it."

Everyone looked at Woo.

"That was obvious to me," Chien An said. "I never believed you had the general's email address. Therefore, it could only have been someone who worked for him, like Ms. Woo."

Woo fidgeted in her chair.

Chien An looked her in the eyes. "You could have escaped unnoticed," Chien An said, turning and pointing to the aircraft outside. "You didn't need to stay in Macau or send the email. Why does the lamb taunt the tiger?"

"I expected General Chao to come here instead of Captain Win. When he did, I planned to shoot him with this," she said, removing a handgun from under the napkin on her lap.

"Where did you get that?" Chien An asked, surprised at what he saw.

"From a friend in Macau. To answer your question, the lamb needs to kill the tiger so that she doesn't hide in fear for the rest of her life. With the tiger's resources, it would eventually find and kill the lamb. Unfortunately, Chao sent someone in his place."

"You taunted the general."

"I couldn't get him to come after me at a time and place of my choice unless I got under his skin, which is why I phoned him twice, took his money for information I never delivered, and didn't answer his calls."

"You phoned him twice?" Tamala asked.

"Once in the restroom after we arrived at the club, and once while I was in the small business office."

Tamala shook his head.

"How much money?" Nabar asked.

"Ten million dollars."

"After conning him out of that much money, I am surprised that he didn't come here and put a bullet in you."

"We're grateful for everything you've done," Wayan said, looking at Chien An. "Do you want us to wait and give a statement to the authorities?"

"Sadly, the Macau authorities are overworked. I'm taking the captain to Beijing where I can get a more determinative autopsy."

As he said this, the captain was being lifted into a body bag by two very large men.

The attractive woman approached the general and told him that someone was coming to clean the blood off the carpet and chairs, and that she'd made the arrangements in Beijing.

"What do you plan to do with General Chao?" Woo asked.

"I'll deal with him in my way," was the cryptic answer.

"In other words, your plans for General Chao are none of our concern."

"My suggestion is that you all live your life as if he doesn't exist."

They watched through the terminal's windows as Chien An boarded an unmarked aircraft. Going up the ramp behind him were the ex-receptionist and two large men carrying a body bag. Minutes later, the plane was airborne.

"I'm next," Woo said after seeing the co-pilots standing beside the stairways to the two aircraft on the tarmac. After getting her wheeled carry-on, she stopped beside Wayan. "If you need to contact me, send a message to this email address using these one-time pads in sequential order," she said, handing them and a piece of paper to him. "The code is unbreakable if you don't reuse a pad. After you've sent the message, destroy it."

"I know how they work."

"Then I guess the only thing left is to say goodbye," she replied, giving Wayan a peck on the cheek before walking out the sliding exit door and onto the tarmac without looking back.

"Strangely, I'll miss her," Wayan said.

"Wipe the lipstick off your cheek," Eka responded after touching it with her finger and smearing the imprint left by Woo. "If you get lonely, look at the reminders she left on your skin."

"And on mine," Tamala added.

They grabbed their bags and headed to their aircraft, which was the Citation X. Five minutes later, it was roaring down the runway.

General Chao's first clue that his plan fell apart was when 25 secret police from the Ministry of State Security burst into his offices and arrested his staff. Sparing him the humiliation of being handcuffed and perp-walked with the others to one of three waiting vans, Chien An's aide took Chao out a side exit and escorted him to a black Audi A6. Placed in the back seat between two stout men wearing a black suit and tie, he was driven to a discrete entrance into the August 1st building and brought by private elevator to Chien An's office on the top floor.

As this was happening, plainclothes MSS agents raided the clearinghouse and arrested the six people inside. They were brought to an unmarked Chinese military aircraft, flown to Beijing, and taken to the same facility as Chao's staff.

As General Hulin Chao entered Chien An's office, he displayed no emotion. He executed a crisp salute, which the general returned, and was directed to a seat at a small conference table. The general sat in the chair across from him and slid the black leather folder he was carrying to Chao, who ignored it.

"You're a thief, opportunist, and murderer," Chien An said. "You set up personal enterprises, purchased businesses, and conducted non-sanctioned illegal activities throughout Asia. In addition, you kept part of the money you laundered for yourself and an entity you refer to as The Organization."

"I used my money, and not the PRCs, to make these investments."

"You already have a job. Military regulations demand exclusivity of employment and require written pre-approval of outside investments by your commanding officer, which is me. You violated both regulations. But you knew that."

"I may have been lax in obtaining your permission, but the money that my partners and I invested is ours. I'm no thief."

"The folder in front of you documents billions of dollars that flow into the coffers of The Organization - an entity in which you're a partner. Most of that is from money-laundering fees. But you've told me and others that you're paying outside agents for this service."

"I am using an outside agent. The Organization launders the money and charges the exact fee as other agents. There is no thievery. The agent fee is a cost of doing business no matter who it's paid to."

"It's a scheme. There shouldn't be a fee because it's an internal function run by government employees. It's all documented in that folder."

Chao opened it. After looking through several documents, some of which seemed to be sticky, he put the papers back inside and slid the folder across the table to Chien An.

"What are your intentions?"

"You're relieved of command and under house arrest. I'll deal with your staff separately."

"Rethink what you're doing. It'll take you a year to reconstruct my operation without guidance from my staff and me. You'll need to wire tens of billions to keep North Korea afloat during that interval."

"The money laundering won't stop. Your staff will be back at work this afternoon, although much poorer, since I'll give them a choice of either returning the money that they've been paid in addition to their government salary or face a firing squad. I'm betting they'll take my offer."

"Who will replace me?"

"The vice-minister of finance. His ministry has stringent monetary controls, so what occurred on your watch will never happen again."

Chao's fingers hurt and began turning purple, indicating a lack of blood flow. He couldn't feel or bend them.

Seeing what was happening, Chien An got up and stood behind Chao's chair. Removing the Sharpie from his pocket, he uncapped it and ran the felt tip around the general's neck. In extreme agony from the lack of blood flow to his fingers, Chao couldn't offer any resistance. When Chien An finished, he recapped the applicator, put it in his pocket, and returned to his chair.

"Clever," Chao said, his head wavering as if he was trying to stay awake. Ten seconds later, his lifeless body fell out of his chair and onto the floor.

Chien An went back to his desk, took a sip of cold tea from his cup, and put on a pair of latex gloves. Placing the black leather folder into a plastic sack, he put it in the two-feet-tall brown paper bag beside his desk, where he placed all classified documents he read and wanted to destroy. The gloves followed. At the end of the day, his aide would take it, after leaving a fresh bag, to the furnace in the building's basement and watch as it turned to ash.

Opening his door, he told his aide to summon a doctor because General Chao had a heart attack.

Returning to his office, he looked down at the body. Chao's mouth was open as if gasping for breath, and his eyes were fixed in a permanent stare.

"That's a better death than you deserved," Chien An said in a low voice.

General Min Kang was in meltdown. Checking his country's bank accounts, he discovered they were empty. Not only were they empty, but his offshore accounts and that of Kim Jong-un's family were as well. Because only he and a few others had the authority to move this money, it didn't take a genius to figure out that the blame would be placed on him. Making things even worse, the empty accounts meant that there was no money for the upcoming purchase. He needed to find out what happened and rectify it before the supreme leader found out. Time wasn't on his side because he knew that Kim Jong-un was addicted to knowing how much cash was in the bank and constantly checked the country's accounts and that of his family.

Pacing his office, Kang dialed Chao for the third time in a minute, only to have his call go unanswered. "Shi-bal," he said, slamming the phone on his desk as four athletic-looking men in suits, who Kang recognized as members of the State Security Department, or SSD, North Korea's secret police, entered his office.

"Our great leader would like to speak with you," one of them said as another disarmed Kang, who always wore a sidearm.

The SSD officials escorted him from the building and into the backseat of a North Korean Pyonghwa SUV. With 80 horsepower, which was less than half that of a standard Toyota Camry, the vehicle pulled away from the building with a sound that was not unlike a lawnmower.

They brought Kang to the Ryongsong presidential complex and into Kim Jong-un's fortified office. He and the athletic four men escorting him waited 20 minutes for the president, supreme ruler, or whatever he called himself that day to arrive.

Kim Jong-un displayed a sour expression as he walked to his desk. He removed a gun from his top drawer, racked the slide to bring the first round from the magazine into the chamber, and put a bullet into each of Kang's kneecaps. Once the general stopped screaming, the supreme leader ordered the four escorts to bring him to the tank.

As they picked him up, Kang tried to get free, but with two gunshot wounds and four men gripping his limbs, it was an exercise in futility.

The tank that Kim Jong-un was referring to was a sixteen-foot-long, five-foot-wide, and four-foot-high, 2000-gallon piranha tank, which rested on the concrete floor. It was stocked with 100 black piranhas, the deadliest of the species, which hadn't been fed in some time. This was intentional because it increased the frenzy with which they went after whatever was thrown into the tank.

After Kang was dumped on the floor in front of the huge tank, the supreme leader put his hands on his hips, bent over, and looked down at him. "Today, you're going to die," he said matter-of-factly. "The only question is how. If you return the money you took, I will put a bullet in your head, and you will suffer no more. If not, you will be thrown into the tank and eaten alive by my piranhas. Where is the money?"

Kang sobbed. "I didn't take it. I can't return what I don't have. It was General Chao! It was Chao!" he screamed.

"I don't doubt that he was your accomplice. Before you arrived," he said in a loud and authoritative voice, "I interrogated one of your staff. He admitted you, Sanadi, Chao, and everyone who worked for what he called The Organization took billions from me. One last time. I want the money you took from me. Now! If I don't get the information from you, I'll get it from General Chao. Believe that."

"I don't have it," he cried.

"Why would you choose to be eaten alive over a bullet?" Kim Jong-un then gave an imperious wave with his right hand. The guards, who knew what this gesture meant because they'd done this before, threw Kang into the tank. One of the men used his phone to film the feeding frenzy that followed, afterward sending it to the supreme leader who would use it to show what happens when someone screwed with him.

CHAPTER 15

I T TOOK FOUR hours and twenty minutes to fly from Macau to the Denpasar International Airport in Bali. Wayan, Eka, Tamala, and Nabar slept in their luxurious seats most of that time, which reclined to a flat position. After they deplaned, Tamala phoned his unit's administrative officer and told him that he and Nabar would return to base later that evening, and he should close their basket leaves, which meant one that was open-ended.

"I should tell your commander what you both did to bring down The Organization," Eka said. "You're heroes and should receive medals."

"I think that should remain our secret forever," Tamala said. "I don't believe our commander, or the local police would believe burning down a warehouse in Bedugul after killing everyone inside, killing a police captain, causing the death of Sanadi, misappropriating a truck, using false passports to get out of Hong Kong and Macau, and so forth is heroic. I believe the word they would use is criminal. Instead of medals, Captain Nabar and I will spend the rest of our military career wearing a different uniform - one with a stenciled number on it."

"Thinking about what you said, the same applies to us."

"And there's the conundrum," Wayan added as he bent over to pick up his carry-on bag, which he'd set down beside him.

"Wayan, can I have a word with you?" Nabar said in a whisper.

"Sure. What is it?"

"Not here." Nabar led him 20 yards from where Eka and Tamala were standing.

"I have a personal question. Is there anything going on between you and Eka?"

"Why do you ask?"

"If there isn't, I'd like to take her out and see what develops. She's an exceptional woman, and I'd like to know her better. I don't want to start down that path if you're a couple."

"Eka and I are terrific friends, but nothing more."

"You must be crazy. She's beautiful, elegant, smart, and has integrity. What's holding you back? Am I missing something?"

"She's everything you described and more. The fact is, I'm still in love with my late wife. I think about her every day. If I entered a relationship, it wouldn't be fair to the other person. It also wouldn't work because I'm in love with another woman - even though she's dead."

"I hope someday I'll have that type of love."

"With the right woman, you will. Ask Eka out."

"Now?"

"Is there a better time?"

Before he could respond, Wayan walked to where she and Tamala were standing.

"Is something up?" Eka asked as she watched them approach. "You both seemed to be deep in conversation."

"Nabar was being a gentleman and asked if we're a couple. If we weren't, he wanted to ask you out. When I said that we were just friends, he told me I was crazy. Does that sum up our conversation?"

Nabar, whose facial expression was not unlike a deer caught in the headlights of an oncoming car, didn't respond.

"Eka, what about it?" Wayan asked.

"I'd love to. I'll give you my phone number," she said with a smile. Removing a piece of paper from her handbag, she wrote her phone number and handed the paper to Nabar.

"Thank you, Eka," the captain responded, coming to life. "I'll text you."

"We need to get moving," Tamala interjected. "We have to go to the main terminal and purchase a ticket on one of the shuttle flights to Jakarta and report back to base."

"Why doesn't the pilot take you there?" Eka asked, pointing to the jet behind them.

"We asked him, but he said he needs to leave as soon as he refuels to pick up a new charter, and Jakarta's in the wrong direction."

"Take care," Wayan said, giving man-hugs to Tamala and Nabar. Eka followed, putting a smile on Nabar's face when she kissed him on the cheek.

"A kiss on the cheek," Wayan said with a grin as he and Eka watched the special forces officers walk across the tarmac.

"At least I'm not wearing lipstick," she responded, referring to the kiss Melis Woo planted on him.

He laughed.

They started walking towards the taxi stand, which was about 50 yards in front of them. On the way, as she was checking her phone messages, she suddenly stopped.

"Listen to this," she said, her voice on edge. Resetting the message, she handed her phone to Wayan, who put it to his ear.

Eka, this is Anna. I'm in serious trouble, and I don't know who else to call. Could you come to the Bulgari and bring Wayan? I'll meet you in the lobby. There's been a double murder at the resort, and I'm going to be the prime suspect. Hurry, time is critical.

AUTHOR NOTES

This is a work of fiction, and the characters within are not meant to depict nor implicate anyone in the actual world. That said, substantial portions of *The Organization*, as stated below, are factual.

The process described for attaining a law degree in Indonesia is accurate. Further information can be obtained from (https://www.lawstudies.com/Indonesia/).

Globally, organ transplants are estimated to generate more than $26.5 billion annually (https://www.grandviewresearch.com/industry-analysis/transplantation-market). Ten percent of organs are obtained illegally or questionably, meaning they're harvested from unwilling or uninformed donors. This group includes the impoverished, uneducated, homeless, donors who see this as a way to escape debt, and those killed to get their organs.

Organ transplants are expensive and profitable. For example, the average price of a heart transplant is $1 million (https://www.howmuchisit.org/heart-transplant-cost/); a liver transplant averages $500,000 (https://costaide.com/liver-transplant-cost/), and a kidney transplant is estimated to be $260,000 (https://health.costhelper.com/kidney-transplant.html). It isn't known how much North Korea derives from the sale of human organs.

Therefore, discard the number that was used for the sake of the storyline. An excellent article to read on organ trafficking can be found at (https://www.acamstoday.org/organ-trafficking-the-unseen-form-of-human-trafficking/).

The procedures used by Desnam in preparing for his sniper shot were taken from an August 19, 2015, Task & Purpose article, *How to Shoot Like a Marine Sniper*, by Michael Lane Smith. You can find this at (https://taskandpurpose.com/gear-tech/how-to-shoot-like-a-marine-sniper/). Information on a rifle scope and adjustments made to "zero" it was taken from the January 6, 2021, Gun University article by Ryan Cleckner. You can find this at (https://gununiversity.com/how-to-adjust-a-riflescope/). The sequence of actions a sniper goes through before taking their shot is not set in stone. It depends on their situation, location, and training. Therefore, procedures vary depending on what article or manual one reads.

As indicated, it's estimated that 2.6 million people live under slavery in North Korea, the vast majority of whom work for the state. Information on this can be found at (https://www.washingtonpost.com/news/worldviews/wp/2018/07/19/north-korea-has-2-6-million-modern-slaves-new-report-estimates/). The U.S. Department of State estimates that there are 100,000 North Korean workers forced into labor overseas and that 80 percent are in Russia or China. Sixty countries have used North Korean forced labor at one time or another (https://www.military.com/daily-news/2018/08/09/north-koreas-slave-labor-exports-are-part-its-broader-business-network.html).

The Sacred Monkey Forest in Ubud is a gorgeous area and well worth a visit. Along with its temple, it's considered holy by the Balinese. However, I inserted the trail, ravine, and stream for the sake of the storyline.

As I noted, if there is a Garden of Eden on earth, it's the Bulgari Resort Bali. The ocean view villas are spectacular and private, to where one feels they're in a private residence and not a resort hotel. The staff is amiable, the food gourmet, and the view magnificent. If you want to put a resort on your bucket list, this is the one. The manager is a very gracious lady who makes everyone feel at home. She and her staff take a personal interest in ensuring that every guest's stay exceeds their expectations. Storywise, she has nothing in common with Anna Bello, nor was she used as the basis for her. Any conclusion that they're the same person is incorrect. Anna Bello is a fictional character who will be the focal point of the next Gunter Wayan-Eka Endah novel, *The Frame*.

The information on gun ownership in Hong Kong is as represented. Citizens may not have firearms unless they're military or police.

The Ritz Hotel Hong Kong is incredible. At 118 stories and in Kowloon, it offers a stunning view of Hong Kong across the harbor. When you're there, visit the Ozone bar, which is on the top floor. It's a beautiful place to have a drink while taking in the view. Like the Bulgari, the hotel manager made my stay memorable. I flew from the Bulgari to the Ritz on my birthday. While on the flight, both managers colluded. When I entered my room, it was festively decorated, and a chocolate cake, which didn't survive long, was in the center of the table. Also on the table was a folder containing the recipe for the calamari appetizer offered at the Bulgari Bali's seaside grill, which I ordered daily and ravenously devoured. Even though I never requested the recipe, it was a thoughtful gesture that indicates both hotel's service levels.

The Peak is the most expensive real estate in Asia, with residences secluded behind heavy landscaping and mountain vegetation. In the visits that I made to Hong Kong to research the locations mentioned in the novel, I also investigated the cost of real estate on The Peak. A mansion, for example, lists for $446 million (https://www.businessinsider.com/most-expensive-home-hong-kong-mansion-photos-2018-9); another for $154 million (https://www.christiesrealestate.com/sales/detail/170-l-78241-f1910280944700023/17-bluff-path-the-peak-hk); a third for $111 million (https://www.christiesrealestate.com/sales/detail/170-l-78241-f1905301021700074/28-barker-road-the-peak-hk).

However, you don't have to be a billionaire to enjoy the view. There's a funicular, or cable-pulled railway designed for steep inclines, that you can take to the top of Victoria Peak. The tram runs from the section of Garden Road near Exchange Square, in an area of Hong Kong that's known as Central. It's the perfect place to watch the sunset.

China's Ministry of State Security (MSS) is accurately portrayed. They're responsible for the foreign intelligence, counterintelligence, and political security of China. Comparatively speaking, the ministry is a composite of both the CIA and the FBI. If the crimes involve national security, it has the same arrest and detention authority as the police.

Quantum encrypted cell phones exist and are used, at least for now, by the government, the military, and anyone else who require, in the words of China Telecom, "absolute security." I obtained this information from a January 7, 2021, article by Coco Feng in *The Star*. This can be found at: (https://www.thestar.com.my/tech/tech-news/2021/01/07/china-telecom-launches-quantum-encrypted-phone-calls-on-smartphones-in-a-new-pilot-programme).

Quantum cryptography is complex, and I didn't explain it in detail because it would divert from the storyline. However, this technology uses quantum mechanics to encrypt and transmit data so that it cannot be hacked. There is an excellent article in QUANTUMXCHANGE that explains the process at the photon level for the technologically inclined. This can be found at: (https://quantumxc.com/quantum-cryptography-explained/#:~:text=Quantum%20cryptography%2C%20or%20quantum%20key,over%20a%20fiber%20optic%20cable.&text=The%20photons%20travel%20to%20a,the%20polarization%20of%20each%20photon.).

My thanks to Julia Layton and Oisin Curran for their September 20, 2018, article in HowStuffWorks, which details the complicated subject of money laundering. You can obtain further information on this subject by going to (https://money.howstuffworks.com/money-laundering8.htm).

According to the United Nations Office on Drugs and Crime (UNODC), the amount of money laundered globally per year is between two to five percent of global GDP, or $800 billion to $2 trillion.

The RSA cryptosystem exists. Not wanting to bog down the storyline by explaining it in detail, I only stated that it was a very secure encryption method. As mentioned, the RSA cryptosystem with a key length of 768 bits has been broken, and one with a key length of 1024 bits may have been. However, according to security researchers, an RSA cryptosystem with a key length of 2048 bits would take a standard computer 300 trillion years to break. A good explanation of RSA can be found in a May 7, 2015, article published by McGuireWoods LLC. You can find this article at (https://www.passwordprotectedlaw.com/2015/05/how-difficult-is-it-to-break-encryption/). Additionally, a June 13,

2019, article by Andreas Baumhof, writing for *Quintessence Labs*, explains how RSA encryption is broken. This can be found at (https://www.quintessencelabs.com/blog/ breaking-rsa-encryption-update-state-art/).

China's Xinjiang Uyghur Autonomous Region is in the country's northwest, where most of the population are Uyghurs, a Turkic (Turkistan) minority ethnic group considered Islamic. Tensions in the region began in the 1950s when the government started promoting cultural unity and punished Uyghur expressions of their cultural heritage. This resulted in severe tension between the Uyghurs, the state police, and Han Chinese, the largest ethnic group in China, which comprises 92 percent of the country's population but only 40 percent in the autonomous region.

To control the situation, China established re-education camps, which are extrajudicial, meaning that those taken there did not have the benefit of a court proceeding. There is no definitive number of Uyghurs ascribed to these camps. However, they're estimated to number into the hundreds of thousands.

As mentioned in the novel, there have been Uyghur attacks in Beijing. However, it was more than seven years before the timeframe referenced in this novel. That incident occurred on October 29, 2013. Five people died in Tiananmen Square in what the police described as a terrorist suicide attack. Three of the dead were terrorists in a 4X4 vehicle, and two were tourists struck by that vehicle. Thirty-eight others were injured. The perpetrators were from China's Xinjiang Uyghur Autonomous Region.

The Lantau Yacht Club exists and is on Discovery Bay, 20 minutes from the Hong Kong International Airport. The clubhouse and marina are magnificent, and membership is by invitation only. For the sake of the storyline, I took liberties with describing the exterior and interior of the clubhouse and the existence of an entry gate. As I required Melis Woo to have both privacy and access to a computer away from the prying eyes of her captors, the creation of business rooms within the clubhouse seemed an excellent way to accomplish this while letting Wayan and his cohorts maintain visual contact with her.

There are several ways to get from Hong Kong to Macau. The cheapest is to take a 34-mile bus ride over the Hong Kong-Zhuhai-Macau bridge and tunnel system, which opened in 2018. The 45-minute ride costs $8. The most expensive is the Sky Shuttle, a commercial helicopter flight that takes 15 minutes and costs $554. My trips to Macau have been on the turbojet ferry. That journey takes an hour and costs $21. It's more relaxing than taking the bus, and it's pleasant being on the water. The only downside in traveling to Macau from Hong Kong and returning is that you must pass through customs and immigration in both places. The lines can be long.

In describing Captain Shum Win's death, I researched near-death experiences from those who'd been shot in the head. An article by Devala Peracini in *Quora* described such an experience and was the basis for what Shum Win felt. You can find the article, translated from Portuguese, at (https://www.quora.com/What-does-it-feel-like-to-get-shot-in-the-head).

Kim Jong-un is purported to have killed numerous generals and aides. The most common methods for dispatching those who suffered his ire is to blast them with an anti-tank gun, incinerate them with a flamethrower, or throw them into a tank filled with hundreds of Piranhas. The piranha tank is reportedly within his residence in Ryongsong, located slightly less than eight miles from the center of Pyongyang. You can find additional details at (https://www.dailymail.co.uk/news/article-7121013/North-Korean-leader-Kim-Jong-executes-general-throwing-piranha-filled-fish-tank.html).

According to a former bodyguard, Kim Jong-un has at least eight residences in and around Pyongyang, connected by tunnels. It's believed the Ryongsong compound is his primary home. As mentioned, it was constructed by Kim -IL-sung, the founder of North Korea. Within its boundaries are a series of artificial lakes, recreational facilities, a shooting range, horse stables, a riding area, a horse racing track, a running track, an athletic field, a 49-foot-by-160-foot swimming pool with a waterslide, and so forth. You get the idea. An electrified fence surrounds the palace, and between it and the residence is a minefield. Vehicle entry into this presidential compound requires passing through several security checkpoints. As mentioned, besides the security forces within the compound, external security is provided by several military units that are stationed nearby. Beneath the compound is a hardened concrete and lead-lined bunker housing Kim Jong-un's office and support facilities.

The five methods by which North Korea gets hard currency are accurately described and were taken from an April 18, 2017, article by Evelyn Cheng. You can find this article at (https://www.cnbc.com/2017/04/18/how-does-north-korea-get-money-to-build-nuclear-weapons.html).

As indicated, North Korea established an arms and ammunition manufacturing plant in Africa, specifically in Namibia. This company is owned by the Korea Mining Development Trading Corporation (KOMID), a subsidiary of the state-owned firm Mansudae Overseas Projects. The factory is in Windhoek, the country's capital. You can find additional information at (https://afripost.net/2016/03/north-korean-built-arms-ammunition-factory-namibia/).

North Korea has been producing illegal drugs since the 1970s when it defaulted on its international debts, and the supreme leader ordered his embassies to self-fund. After that, the state began producing illicit drugs. An excellent piece explaining this, and other illegal activities of the Hermit Kingdom, is the October 5, 2015, *Listverse* article: *10 of North Korea's Top Exports*. This can be found at (https://listverse.com/2015/10/02/10-of-north-koreas-top-exports/). The description of North Korea's cybercrimes is accurate. It's estimated that this activity has generated over $2 billion from hacking both financial institutions and cyber currency exchanges.

North Korea's Yongbyon Scientific Research Center is real and is believed to produce weapons-grade fissile material. It is also the site of the country's plutonium production reactor.

Hospital 301 is located in Beijing and is the PLA's Postgraduate Medicate School. It caters to both Chinese leaders and senior PLA officers. It's believed to have a medical staff of 2,800 and carry out liver, kidney, corneal, blood vessel, and parathyroid transplants.

Unit 61398 is part of the People's Liberation Army and is known to conduct cyber spying for the Chinese government. Located within a 12-story, 130,000 square foot building on Datong Road in Shanghai's Pudong district, 2,000 people are believed to work within this building. Mandiant, an internet security firm, estimates that Unit 61398 has systematically stolen hundreds of terabytes of data from over 141 organizations across 20 industries worldwide. Further information on Unit 61398 can be obtained by going to (https://www.cnn.com/2014/05/20/world/asia/

china-unit-61398/index.html) and (https://www.csmonitor.com/USA/2013/0219/Massive-cyberattacks-from-China-Report-claims-to-expose-secret-Unit-61398).

As referenced, soju is a colorless spirit distilled from rice and various grains. Koreans cannot get enough of it, and the average South Korean drinks 13.7 shots of this liquor per week, making it the most popular alcoholic beverage globally. There are no figures for North Korean consumption of soju, probably because only the elite can afford it.

ACKNOWLEDGMENTS

I want to thank again my extraordinary group of friends who continue to give me the benefit of their opinions and thoughts unselfishly. In many ways, the phrase *it takes a village* applies to writing and publishing a manuscript. I constantly receive suggestions from this group. They're not shy about pointing out holes in the storyline or a character's actions.

Publishing a manuscript is a process. When it's complete, at least from my viewpoint, the editors, proofreader, and cover copy sections get a shot at me. Once I'm through this gauntlet, the manuscript is sent for the print layout, and the cover is designed. If I agree that this is what I want to be printed and the cover reflects the story, I digitally sign the approval forms for the manuscript, cover, and pricing. A day later, Amazon, Barnes & Noble, and so forth have it

One of my friends, Ed Houck, asked what it feels like to get editorial comments. I told him that some editors believe that there are authors, obviously not me, who would be better off taking a home study course in how to be a plumber rather than writing a manuscript - and they're not shy about sharing those opinions. Therefore, having the thickness of an elephant's skin and keeping one's ego in check is requisite for having a manuscript published. That said, having gotten to know the staff of iUniverse over the past decade, I've found their comments and suggestions to be insightful and accurate. In the end, my manuscript reflects their invisible hand, fine-tuning my work. Therefore, thank you to the editorial staff at iUniverse.

My sincere gratitude -

To: Kerry Refkin for her edits and storyline recommendations. Her understanding of the characters and their motivations is extraordinary.

To: The Group - Scott Cray, Dr. Charles and Aprille Pappas, Dr. John and Cindy Cancelliere, Doug and Winnie Ballinger, Alexandra Parra, Ed Houck, Cheryl Rinell, Mark Iwinski, Mike Calbot, and Dr. Meir Daller for continuing to be my sounding boards.

To: Zhang Jingjie for her expertise in finding even the most obscure details requested by me. Her flawless research makes it easy to connect the dots.

To: Dr. Kevin Hunter and Rob Durst, close friends for decades, for explaining to this computer novice, IT and computer-related security issues. If there was a technical error, it's mine.

To: Clay Parker, Jim Bonaquist, and Greg Urbancic. Thank you for the excellent legal advice you provide.

To: Bill Wiltshire. Thanks again for your superb financial and accounting skills.

To: Doug and Winnie Ballinger and Scott and Betty Cray. Your charitable work breathes hope into the lives of countless people. Without it, they would have an existence of destitution and desolation. You're heroes.

To the incredible managers and staff of the Bulgari Hotel Bali and the Ritz Hong Kong. Thank you for your hospitality and for helping me conduct my research.

ABOUT THE AUTHOR

Alan Refkin is the author of eight previous works of fiction, and the co-author of four business books on China, for which he received the Editor's Choice Award for *The Wild Wild East,* and for *Piercing the Great Wall of Corporate China.* In addition to the Wayan Gunter series, the author has published the Matt Moretti-Han Li thrillers and the Mauro Bruno detective series. The author and his wife, Kerry, live in southwest Florida where he is currently working on his next Gunter Wayan novel, *The Frame.* More information on the author, including his blogs and newsletters, can be obtained at *alanrefkin.com.*

Printed in the United States
by Baker & Taylor Publisher Services